Amish by Accident

J.E.B. Spredemann

Blessed Publishing

BOOKS BY J.E.B. SPREDEMANN

AMISH GIRLS SERIES

Joanna's Struggle

Danika's Journey

Chloe's Revelation

Susanna's Surprise

Annie's Decision

Abigail's Triumph

Brooke's Quest

NOVELLAS

Amish by Accident *

To my Best Friends…

Thank you for your love and companionship throughout the years.

Author's Note

It should be noted that the Amish people and their communities differ one from another. There are, in fact, no two Amish communities exactly alike. It is this premise on which this book is written. We have taken cautious steps to assure the authenticity of Amish practices and customs. Both Old Order Amish and New Order Amish are portrayed in this work of fiction and may be inconsistent with some Amish communities.

We, as *Englischers*, can learn a lot from the Plain People and their simple way of life. Their hard work, close-knit family life, and concern for others are to be applauded. As the Lord wills, may this special culture continue to be respected and remain so for many centuries to come.

Unofficial Glossary
of Pennsylvania Dutch Words

Ach – Oh

Ausbund – Amish hymn book

Bloobier – Blueberry

Boppli – Baby

Bopplin – Babies

Bruder – Brother

Dat, Daed – Dad

Dawdi – Grandfather

Denki – Thanks

Der Herr – The Lord

Dochder – Daughter

Dokter – Doctor

Dummkopp – Dummy

Englischer – A non-Amish person

Ferhoodled – Mixed up, Crazy

Fraa – Woman, Wife

Gott – God

Gut – Good

Gross Dawdi – Great Grandfather

Haus – House

Hullo – Hello

Jah – Yes

Kapp – Prayer Cap

Kumm – Come

Lieb – Love

Liede – Song

Mamm – Mom

Mammi – Grandmother

Mein Liewe – My Dear

Mudder – Mother

Nee – No

Ordnung – Rules of the Amish Community

Rumspringa – Running around years

Schweschder – Sister

Vadder – Father

Vorsinger – Song Leader

Wunderbaar – Wonderful

PROLOGUE

Elisabeth Schrock yawned as Minister Fisher's voice droned on and on about how he deemed it necessary for their Amish youth to flee from the things of the world. *You've got to be kidding, right? His boys are some of the most unruly in our district. He must be preaching to his own* kinner. It took everything she had to not snicker and roll her eyes. Of course, his twins were in *Rumspringa* just as she was. *I've heard all this before. It's always the same old thing. The world is wicked; we must live by the rules of the Ordnung...blah, blah, blah.* Her discontent and restlessness had been growing daily, along with her rebellious attitude. She was sure that if she had to sit through this for another Sunday, she would burst.

She reached inside her hidden apron pocket and clutched the letter she'd received from her best friend, Mattie Riehl. Mattie left her conservative Mennonite community a year earlier and now worked in a fancy skyscraper in New York City. She said she'd met a wonderful *Englisch* beau and is happier now than she'd ever been. Mattie encouraged Elisabeth to come visit and even offered to share her apartment if she decided to stay long-term. Oh, how she longed for freedom! She was aching to escape the monotony and endless rules and restrictions of the church. *I'm going to do it!* she decided resolutely.

A cough drew her attention to the men's side of the room. She glanced up to see her handsome beau, Luke Beiler, looking at her curiously. He must've sensed her musing and raised his eyebrows in question. *How am I going to leave Luke? He's ready to join the church and be baptized, but I just can't do it right now. There's too much out there that I haven't seen or experienced. I know that if I agree to be baptized this fall with Luke, he'll ask me to marry him.* Elisabeth hung her head. Indeed, leaving would be the most difficult decision of her life. Nevertheless, she was determined to do it. Today.

Leaving his hot coffee, Luke stood up from the breakfast table when Jacob Schrock beckoned him to the porch outside. It was indeed strange for Elisabeth's brother to be visiting on a Monday morning, with all the chores he had to tend to and what not. But Jacob's sober countenance gave pause for concern. His friend held out an envelope to him. It was Elisabeth's handwriting. *For Luke.* He searched Jacob's face for a sign as to what the contents might be, but Jacob kept his gaze on the wooden boards beneath his feet. Without a word, Luke opened the letter that would forever change his life.

2

Luke,

I'm sorry. I just don't feel like I belong here with the Plain people in Paradise anymore. Whether I will come back or not, I do not know. Please do not try to find me.

Elisabeth

Heartbroken. It was the only word that could describe Luke Beiler as he let Elisabeth's letter slip through his fingers onto the hard wooden floor. All his hopes and dreams for the future, dashed into a million pieces with just a smidgen of ink on plain white paper.

ONE

Two years later...

"Please listen to me, Brianna. This is important," Carson urged.

Brianna Mitchell looked down at their intertwined hands, and then glanced at her watch. "Carson, we've been over this before. I'm happy that you found religion, really I am. I can see that it's helped you and made you a better person. But I'm just not ready for anything like that. Besides, I really have to go. My plane leaves at four, and Heidi will be expecting me."

Something inside Carson told him to push the subject, so he continued, "Won't you just listen for a few minutes? God wants to share His amazing love with you."

Brianna abruptly held up her hand to silence him. "I love you, Carson. But I really do need to go. Maybe we'll talk about this some other time, okay?" She leaned over and placed a kiss on his cheek, hoping to distract him. He acquiesced and pulled her into his arms for a warm embrace, then gently brushed his lips against hers.

"I'll miss you. Have a nice trip." As Brianna walked out the door, an uneasy feeling surged in the pit of Carson's stomach. "May God be with you, Brianna," he whispered softly.

Brianna frantically searched through her purse one more time, a helpless look etched across her face. *No, it has to be here!*

"I'm really sorry, Miss. But we can't let you board without your passport." The ticket agent stomped her foot impatiently, eyeing the long line of travelers behind Brianna. "Next!"

Brianna sighed. *I'll take that as my cue to leave.*

Realization suddenly dawned on her. She'd forgotten that she switched out handbags when packing up her clothing for the trip. Without thinking, she'd grabbed her usual purse, forgetting that she packed the one for the trip in her carry-on bag. Her identification, passport, tickets, and everything important was in her *other* purse – the one sitting in her bedroom at present. *I can't believe I left my luggage at home. How could I be so stupid! I guess that's what I get for leaving in such a rush. Now, I'll have to go back home and rebook my flight.*

She knew Heidi would be disappointed; they'd been planning this trip for two years. Her friend had come to the United States as a foreign exchange student her senior year of high school and they instantly became close friends. They were both excited that Brianna would be visiting Heidi in Germany, her home country.

She walked out of the airport and hailed the first taxi she saw; thankfully she still had some money in the purse she carried.

Brianna watched as a blue and yellow taxi cab veered to where she stood on the sidewalk and screeched to a halt. She hopped in and slid to the middle of the seat.

"Where to, lady?" the cab driver called over his shoulder.

Brianna quickly gave him the address and he set the meter. She looked out the window, watching the tall buildings pass by. People dashed to and fro, everyone seemingly in their own little world. A hot dog vendor handed a small boy a foot-long frank and she smiled as the boy's eyes lit up with sheer delight. She enjoyed the distractions. They helped to take her mind off of other things that pressed for her attention. Like her missed flight. Or, worse yet, Carson's new-found fascination with religion.

"I'm Jimmy," the driver introduced himself, glancing at Brianna in his rearview mirror. She nodded politely, not wanting to engage in conversation. "Hey, anyone ever told you about the Lord?"

Oh no, not this again. "I really don't want to talk about it right now, so if you could please just get me where I need to go." She regretted her rudeness, but she was not in the mood to discuss spiritual matters with a perfect stranger.

"Thought I'd try." The cabbie shrugged. "Do you mind?" he asked as he pointed to the radio.

Brianna shook her head. *Anything would be better than discussing religion.*

"Hey, listen to this!" He turned up the volume and a news-woman's voice sounded over the airwaves.

"Preliminary reports are now coming in for Flight 245 from JFK International en route to Paris. As we have just confirmed with the FAA, American Airlines Flight 245 has gone down over the Atlantic Ocean just ten minutes ago. Reports are still coming in, but it appears there are no survivors. I repeat: American Airlines Flight 245 to Paris has gone down over the Atlantic Ocean..." the news report continued.

"My flight! That was my flight! I was supposed to be on that plane." *No survivors.* Brianna's hands shook as she came to grips with reality. Her head started spinning and she began hyperventilating.

"Hey, calm down, lady. Are you alright?" Jimmy turned to look at her in the back seat.

"Watch out!" she screamed, as their taxi veered into oncoming traffic. Brianna panicked as a huge red semi-truck headed straight toward them. Everything suddenly went black.

Elisabeth blew out a breath, causing her bangs to flutter. She peered around the small front office where she worked with two other women. The office was bright and cheerful, probably to cater to the younger clients who visited the private dental practice. Once again, she eyed the large poster on the wall and smiled. "Brush after every meal!" the sign ordered, depicting a small boy and girl with shiny white teeth holding toothbrushes. She almost laughed, thinking of her younger brother, Jacob. Oh, how he'd hated brushing his teeth when he was small!

I wonder how Mamm and Dat are doing. And Luke. How did he react when he found the letter I left for him? Shocked, to be sure. Has he found someone else? Is he married? A pang of regret crept into her heart, but she quickly dismissed it. After all, this was the life she'd chosen. She would be content and look toward the future with hopeful expectation. The past was behind her now and nothing could change or undo the choices she'd made. Not that she'd want anything to be different.

The telephone rang, jolting her back to the present. "Family Dental, may I help you?" She listened as the man on the other line detailed his needs, and then scheduled an appointment for him on the computer in front of her. "Your appointment is for Friday at four o'clock, Mr. Welch. And since this is your first visit, you'll need to come about fifteen minutes early to fill out the necessary paperwork. Thank you, and have a nice day." She set the receiver back into its cradle and looked up at the clock on the wall. Five o'clock, quitting time.

After maneuvering through the congested New York traffic, Elisabeth finally arrived at the small Mexican restaurant that Mattie had chosen. She'd never even known of such a thing growing up, but since moving to the city she had come to love the delicious south-of-the-border flavors. She often tried to duplicate it at home in the apartment she and Mattie shared, but it never tasted quite the same as the authentic fare. Her mouth watered as she envisioned the large bean burrito she usually ordered: beans, cheese, rice, shredded cabbage, avocado, fresh salsa with plenty of cilantro, and lime to squeeze onto each bite.

"You made it before I did this time." Mattie smiled as she dropped her purse and took a seat across from Elisabeth.

"Traffic didn't seem as bad today," Elisabeth said as she sipped her ice water and glanced at the large sombrero hanging from the ceiling. "I already ordered for both of us."

"Great! I don't know about you, but I'm starving." Mattie placed the menu back onto the table. "So, how was work? Any cute guys come in and sweep you off your feet today?"

Elisabeth giggled. "You're silly, Mattie. No, not today."

"I'm a helpless romantic, what can I say? Richard brought me flowers today, isn't that sweet?" Mattie's face fairly beamed with contentment.

"Isn't that twice this month already? Has he hinted at anything?" Elisabeth feared to ask.

"Marriage? Well, we have been dating for over two years now. The subject has come up a few times. I think he's trying to summon enough nerve to ask me." She twirled her shoulder-length brown hair around her finger.

"So, if he does ask, what will we do about the apartment? We can barely make the payments right now. I surely wouldn't be able to pay the rent on my own," Elisabeth said with obvious concern.

"I don't think you have anything to worry about, Lis. Even if he does ask me to marry him, I'm sure the wedding won't be for at least six months," Mattie asserted. "We'll figure something out between now and then."

"Will you invite anyone from home? I mean, I know that your folks probably won't come but how about your brothers and sisters? I know that Rebekah would want to see you get married."

Mattie swallowed the lump in her throat and swiped a tear from her cheek. "I'm sorry. It's just that I haven't thought of home in so long. I miss it sometimes, you know. It's not easy living without your family, especially where we come from, *jah?*"

"*Jah,*" Elisabeth replied in their native Pennsylvania Dutch and squeezed her friend's hand. "I miss it sometimes too."

"I'm glad you're here with me. I think I might have gone back by now if it wasn't for you. Thank you for coming, I hope you've been happy here."

"I have," Elisabeth said before sinking her teeth into her scrumptious dinner.

TWO

*B*rianna attempted to open her eyes, but her eyelids refused to cooperate. She heard the faint sounds of unfamiliar voices and the annoying squeaking of a wheel. A loud beep startled her and her eyes flew open. Her eyes roamed the room, but it all seemed so foreign. *Where am I?* She surmised, by the white gown covering her body, that she was in a hospital. *What happened?* She tried to recall what had happened, but her mind came up blank.

"Oh good, you're finally awake." A friendly African-American woman smiled down at her. "I'm just gonna check your blood pressure, then I'll send the doctor in to speak with you." The woman wrapped the cuff around Brianna's arm and began to squeeze the attached rubber pump causing the cuff to constrict on her arm. She let the rubber bulb go and Brianna felt her arm relaxing. "Looks good." The nurse turned and headed out the door.

"Wait!" Brianna called after her, but it was too late.

Brianna's eyelids grew heavy and she fell back to sleep.

Sometime later, she was awakened again and a man in a long white coat appeared. She glanced up at the fifty-something-year-old man as he surveyed her chart and determined that the doctor was probably rather good-looking when he was younger. His salt-and-pepper hair gave him an aire of sophistication and accented his sharp facial features nicely.

"So, Miss Jane Doe, do you have a real name?" His kind blue eyes peered over the top of his wire-rimmed spectacles.

"Yes, I'm…uh…I'm…" Her voice trailed off as she racked her brain. *Surely, I know my own name!* She looked up at the doctor helplessly. "I…I can't remember."

"That's all right." The man gently patted her hand. "You've been through a lot. Sometimes it takes the brain a while to re-cover. Temporary memory loss is quite common in brain inju-ries. I'll have my intern come in and give you some tests." He arose from the chair and started toward the door.

"Wait! Please tell me what happened. Why am I here? Why do I have a brain injury?" Brianna pleaded for answers.

"I'll have the nurse come in and explain it all to you. Right now, just relax and try to get some rest." He smiled at her before exiting the room.

Easy for you to say, you know who you are! Relax? She sat up in her bed and swung her legs over the side, determined to stand up and go find some answers. When her feet hit the floor and she lifted herself from the bed, her legs became shaky and began to buckle. Panic set in and she quickly reached back to the bed for stability. Resigned and out of breath, she hoisted herself back onto the bed and decided it would be best to wait for the nurse. Brianna yawned and couldn't resist the delicious pull of sleep as her heavy eyelids draped shut.

"Luke, did you hear me?" Sarah Anne Yoder asked, becoming more impatient every minute.

"*Ach*, I'm sorry, Sarah. What did you say?" Luke turned his attention to the beautiful girl sitting next to him. She was very pretty indeed, with facial features from both her German Amish father and German-Mexican Amish mother. She was a nice girl, too. In fact, any boy from their district would be happy sitting next to Sarah Anne. But she wasn't Elisabeth.

"I asked if you plan on attending the youth gathering next Saturday. My parents will be hosting it, so it will be a lot of fun," she said excitedly, flashing her perfect white teeth.

Luke stared out across Millers' Pond as they ate the picnic lunch that Sarah Anne had prepared for the occasion. "*Jah*, I'll probably go." He shrugged half-heartedly.

"Are you all right, Luke? You don't seem too enthusiastic." She frowned.

"No, I'm fine. Just thinkin' is all." He scooted closer to her and draped his arm around her shoulder.

Sarah Anne smiled up at him, and then gasped as he bent his head and leaned in to kiss her.

15

Luke pulled Sarah close and eagerly kissed her on the lips. As he closed his eyes, he allowed his thoughts to drift back to Elisabeth. His hands caressed her soft brown hair that flowed down around her shoulders and her sweet lips pressed to his. He paused for a breath and whispered, "I love you, Beth." Immediately his lovely vision ended as Sarah Anne abruptly pushed him away, hurt written on her pretty face.

"Beth?" Sarah's voice screeched. "How dare you, Luke Beiler! I thought you actually cared for *me*, when all along you've been fantasizing about Elisabeth Schrock. I figured after she left you two years ago that you'd be over her by now, but obviously I was wrong." Sarah Anne wiped away a tear and stomped off in a huff, leaving Luke dazed and confused on the picnic quilt.

Ach, he chided himself. "I'm sorry, Sarah. Come back." But Sarah Anne picked up her pace, headed toward home and away from him as quickly as possible. He pounded his fists on the ground in frustration. *Will I ever be able to get Elisabeth out of my head? She left me. She chose the* Englisch *life over a life with me.* Luke sighed, and then sent up a desperate prayer. "Lord, if there's any way Elisabeth and I can get back together, please let it happen. I know I was angry with her for leaving and that I said I'd never be able to forgive her. But I'm stuck, Lord. I love her. I've tried courting other girls, but it's just not working. I need her."

16

Carson glanced in the mirror on his sun visor before stepping out of the car. He walked up to the office building and cringed before opening the door. Oh, how he hated going to the dentist! Ever since he got his first cavity filled when he was seven years old, he'd loathed the place. He'd sworn off candy for the rest of his life after going through the torture chamber, as he called it.

Hopefully this dentist would be gentler. He'd discussed his fear of dentistry with a co-worker one day and she recommended Family Dental. She claimed that she couldn't even feel the shots given by the dentist! Whether he believed her or not was beside the point. He was so intrigued he figured he'd at least give this dentist a try.

Fortunately, today he'd just be getting x-rays and a cleaning. He strolled up to the receptionist's desk with nervous anticipation. Nobody greeted him, so he gingerly rang the small brass bell atop the counter. When a woman rounded the corner with a file folder in her hand, he felt as if the wind had been knocked out of him and he nearly fainted.

"Brianna?" His eyes widened as he gripped the counter to steady himself.

"Brianna?" The woman blinked in confusion, then realized the intent of his question. "Oh. Uh…no, my name is Elisabeth."

"I…I'm sorry. It's just that you look so much like her." Carson's hands trembled. He took a deep breath and squeezed his eyes shut to prevent a tear from forming. He turned back to the receptionist. "But, I guess you can't be her." The realization that Brianna was gone forever grieved his heart once again. He raked his hands through his hair, regaining his composure, trying his best not to stare but failing miserably.

"Did you have an appointment today, sir?" the receptionist asked, seemingly unmoved by his obvious attention.

"Oh, yes. Welch." He cleared his throat. "Carson Welch. It's my first appointment. The woman on the phone said that I'd have to fill out some paperwork, so I came in a little early." He had a hard time concentrating while Elisabeth stood right in front of him. His eyes trailed her every move as she walked toward a stack of files and returned with one marked 'WE' in bright orange stickers. She pulled out some blank forms and handed them to him. A chill ran up his arms when they unintentionally brushed fingers.

Carson returned to the waiting room and took a seat on one of the plush burgundy chairs. He stared down at the papers on his lap, wondering how he'd focus enough to fill them out. *Did Brianna have a twin?* He'd never heard her mention it, but he couldn't help but wonder now. He looked back over to the receptionist's desk, but Elisabeth had disappeared behind the filing shelves once again. As he forced himself to concentrate, he realized the clipboard was missing a pen and he'd left his own in the car. He sighed and returned to the front desk, clearing his throat.

Her beautiful face appeared around the corner once again. "May I help you, Mr. Welch?" Her bright blue eyes shined the way Brianna's used to.

He gave her a warm smile. "Carson, please. Mr. Welch is my father."

She laughed and it all but brought him to tears. "All right, Carson. Do you need something?"

Was he imagining it or was she flirting with him? "A pen. The clipboard is missing a pen and I left mine in the car."

"Of course, here you go." She smiled again.

Carson took the pen and winked at her before turning back to his seat. *I have to figure out a way to spend some time with her. What if I never see her again?* He thought his racing heart might beat right out of his chest as he came up with a plan.

After Carson disappeared into the back office, Elisabeth took her seat once again. It wasn't every day that an attractive man her age walked in to their dental office. It was quite rare, actually. The normal clientele consisted of mostly children and older adults. She guessed by the absence of a ring on his finger that he wasn't married. Not to mention he'd winked at her. But it was peculiar the way he stared at her, as if he thought he knew her.

"I think he likes you." Her friend Marilyn smiled, as she sat at her desk in the corner.

Immediately Elisabeth's cheeks blushed. "He *is* cute."

Her other co-worker laughed, playfully slapping her shoulder. "Cute? Girl, that man is a drop-dead gorgeous babe. If I were thirty years younger…" Connie's voice drifted off.

Elisabeth smiled, shaking her head at her friends' straightforwardness. She answered a few more phone calls and scheduled appointments as quitting time drew near. She'd just returned a file to its proper place when a smiling Carson strolled up to Connie's desk holding a new toothbrush. Elisabeth looked around, but her co-worker was nowhere in sight.

"Connie must've stepped out. Do you need another appointment?" Elisabeth asked.

"As a matter of fact, I've got a cavity that needs to be filled." He grimaced, and then signaled her near with his finger. He leaned down to her ear as if he harbored a delicious secret. "Tell me something. Is it true that the shots here don't hurt?"

Elisabeth almost laughed, and then noticed true concern in his eyes. "It's true. Although, I've only had one so I can't give you an expert opinion."

"Whew!" He swiped the back of his hand across his forehead. "Am I happy to hear that. I had a really bad experience as a boy and I've been frightened of dentists ever since."

She suppressed a chuckle and tried to give him a reassuring smile.

"You're laughing at me." He feigned offense, but his eyes sparkled. "Just for that, you'll have to accompany me for coffee after work."

She couldn't believe this stranger's boldness. "I'm afraid that's not in my job description. Besides, I might get fired if I schedule dates with the patients while I'm working."

"Hmm...when do you get off work?" He glanced down at his Rolex.

"Five minutes." She blushed, suddenly shy now.

"I'll just have to wait until you get off work, then I'll ask you. Problem solved," he said triumphantly.

She smiled, and then sat up straight when Connie came into the room. "Here is your appointment, Mr. Welch." Resuming her professional demeanor, she handed him a business card with his appointment time written on it.

"I'll see you soon." He winked and sauntered out the door.

THREE

*B*rianna sat in yet another hospital room, waiting for the physical therapist to arrive. She noted the exercise equipment that worked every muscle in the body in the large room. Today would be just like the other days she'd undergone therapy – painful. She cringed just thinking of it. But like the therapist had encouraged her, this was just temporary; one necessary step on the road to recovery that would eventually make her whole. Hopefully.

That was the problem though. Even if she made a complete physical recovery, her brain would most likely never fully recover. The doctor had said that her type of memory loss – Retrograde Amnesia – could be recovered in *some* cases. But unfortunately, a full recovery was highly unlikely. He said that there was no known treatment for Retrograde Amnesia.

What kind of life would she have? Would she ever be able to remember her past life and who she was? An overwhelming feeling of depression clouded her mind as she realized she might always be known as Jane Doe. *Doesn't anybody care about me? Why has nobody come looking for me?* Surely somebody was out there – a mother or father – or perhaps siblings. But she'd been hospitalized for nearly three months and not one soul had come. Fortunately she didn't have to think about it all the time, though. The pharmaceutical medications they'd given her assured her of a good night's rest. They helped to dull the pain and the feelings of rejection and loneliness. There had to be at least one person in this world who cared about her, but where were they?

The nurse explained to her how she'd come to be in the hospital. A car accident. Apparently she was in a taxi that collided head-on with a large semi-truck. She had been the lucky one, the nurse had said. The cab driver was dead at the scene. She had no identification on her, so nobody knew who she was. Police reports had been checked for missing persons, but the two that matched her description had already been positively identified.

So, here she was at the hospital. All alone. What would happen when she was better and they released her? Where would she go? She couldn't just walk out onto the street with no home to go to. Frightened could not even begin to describe her state of mind. She was desperate. Lonely. Craving for someone to claim her as their own.

"All right, Miss Doe. Are you ready to do this again?" the enthusiastic trainer called out as she entered the room.

"Ready as I'll ever be, I guess." Brianna shrugged.

"Have you been walking like I recommended?"

"Yes, I have. I love to take the elevator to the sixth floor to look at the newborn babies." Her sad face perked up.

"Ah yes, the nursery is always a favorite." The woman smiled as well. "Finally, a smile. I was beginning to think you'd forgotten how to smile too."

"No, I haven't. This isn't exactly my favorite time of day." She grimaced.

"Yes, I'm afraid I don't make many friends around here." The trainer chuckled. "Let's get started, shall we?"

Mattie fairly bounced through the door Saturday evening, grinning from ear to ear. "Guess –"

"Don't say it!" Elisabeth said excitedly. "Richard asked you to marry him!"

"Yes!" Mattie beamed.

Elisabeth enveloped her friend in a warm embrace, sharing her joy. "Oh Mattie, I'm so happy for you. So when's the big day?"

Mattie set her purse and keys down on the small end table beside their couch. "That's the thing, Lis. He wants to get married soon."

Elisabeth swallowed hard, uncertainty filling her mind. "Soon? How soon?"

"Three months. But I'm sure we can find you a roommate between now and then." Mattie tried to reassure her friend. "Is there someone at work who might be interested?"

"No, I don't think so. Besides, I don't think I'd want to live with most of them. They party every weekend." She shook her head. "And the ones that I would consider are older and already have a place of their own."

"What about Carson?" Mattie raised her eyebrows and smiled.

"Carson? You'd want me to *live* with Carson?" Her eyes grew big as saucers at the unthinkable suggestion. Amish or not, she would never live with a boyfriend outside of wedlock.

"No, that's not what I mean." Mattie laughed. "Are the two of you serious? Is it possible that *he* might propose?"

Elisabeth shook her head. "We've only been dating for a couple of months. I really do like him, but I think he still has some issues to deal with."

"Like?"

"Like his old girlfriend Brianna. Remember how I told you that she died in that terrible plane crash over the ocean?" Elisabeth continued on when Mattie nodded, "The only reason he was attracted to me is because I look like her. I just hope he likes me for me, not for Brianna."

"I see."

"I don't know if he's completely over her yet." She shook her head.

"I'm not sure if you can ever be completely over a loved one dying." Mattie sighed. "How about you? Are you completely over Luke? *He's* still alive."

"I think so. I mean, I did care for him. But I think he cared for me more. I wonder how he's doing." Elisabeth blew out a breath. "If I had stayed, we'd probably be married by now."

"Sounds like you might have some regrets." Mattie lifted her eyebrows as if questioning her friend.

"No. No regrets. I'm happy here. I'm glad I met Carson; he's a really great guy. He's a Christian. And incredibly handsome." Elisabeth smiled. "If he ever did want to marry me..." Her thoughts trailed off for a few seconds. "I think because of what happened with Brianna, he wants to take things slow."

"Don't you think he's taking it slow for your benefit? He probably knows you're apprehensive because he told you that you reminded him of his lost love. But I would think that he's probably already decided to like you for who *you* are, not for who Brianna was," Mattie offered.

"I hope so."

"Well, perhaps you should ask him then. Be honest with him about your feelings," Mattie suggested. "What have you got to lose?"

"You're right," Elisabeth agreed. "Maybe I'll ask him after church tomorrow."

"That was a convicting sermon, wasn't it?" Carson lifted his brow, and then sank his teeth into his veggie burger.

"Yes, it was." Elisabeth sighed.

"Is something the matter? It seems as if you're a million miles away." He set his burger down for a moment and gave her his undivided attention.

"When we first met, you said that I reminded you of Brianna." She took a breath and continued on, "I…I was just wondering if that's the only reason you're dating me."

Carson's brow furrowed in concern and he reached for Elisabeth's hand. "I admit that is what drew me to you in the first place, Elisabeth. But you must know that I care for *you*. And while you and Brianna may look alike, it is obvious you are two very different people."

"That's good to hear. You've seemed reticent for some reason."

"I admit that I have regrets about my relationship with Brianna. The last time I saw her I was frustrated with her. I tried to share the Gospel with her, but she just wouldn't listen. I think she just probably thought that she'd live forever. And now, it's too late for her." Carson sighed, obviously grieved. "I've harbored anger towards her. If only she hadn't been so stubborn. I fear she's in Hell now."

Elisabeth looked down at their intertwined fingers. "I'm sorry. I had no idea."

Carson brightened a bit, giving a half-smile. "I don't regret my relationship with you, though. As a matter of fact, I was hoping we could spend more time together? I want to know everything about you. You intrigue me."

Elisabeth laughed. "I've never thought of myself as intriguing, but I think I'd enjoy spending more time with you. Especially since I'll probably have more free time now that Mattie and Richard are getting married. I'm sure they'll want to spend extra time together."

Carson smiled. "They are? That's great! Be sure to tell Mattie congratulations for me. When's the big day?"

"In a few months." She frowned.

"For some reason, you don't seem too thrilled."

"Oh no, I'm happy for Mattie. It's just that she and I are roommates."

"Ah, I see. You're worried about finding another roommate." He caught on. "We could ask around at church. Perhaps there's a college student or someone else who's looking to rent."

"That's a great idea! I don't know why I never thought of that before." Elisabeth smiled now.

"I guess we make a good team." Carson smiled, looking down at their now cold food. "We should probably eat now."

Elisabeth agreed, and took a bite of her salad with a renewed sense of confidence.

FOUR

Luke donned his hat and approached Elisabeth's brother, Jacob, after church on Sunday. "Hey Jacob, have you heard anything about Elisabeth?" he asked as they lifted the wooden bench to haul it outside for the meal.

"*Nee.*" Jacob glowered. "I'm sorry, Luke. It just doesn't seem as if Elisabeth will be coming back to our people. She's chosen a different way."

"How can you be sure she won't return?" Luke challenged, refusing to give up.

"No letters, no phone calls. It's pretty clear she doesn't want to be involved with any of us anymore." Jacob shook his head in shame. "If I were you, Luke, I'd move on."

Luke blew out a frustrated breath, wanting to cry. "I've tried to, Jacob. My mind won't let me forget her. I've tried courting other *maedel.* For some reason my heart just can't let go."

"I don't mean to discourage you, Luke. But how long are you willing to wait for her? She may never come home. What if she's already married to an *Englischer*? I'd hate to see a fine Amish man like you end up without a wife and *kinner*."

Luke's heart ripped in two at the thought of Elisabeth married to someone else. "You're a *gut* friend, Jacob. *Denki* for your advice." Luke patted Jacob's back, and then walked toward his buggy with his shoulders slumped and head down. He was no longer in the mood for fellowship, he just wanted to be alone.

Brianna peered through the large window into the sea of plexiglass cradles. Each infant, so small and precious, belonged to someone. Someone who cared for them. Someone who loved them. Brianna sniffled and turned away, unable to bear the thought that she had no one. The pain wrenched her heart. She couldn't stop the flow of tears, even though others now stood on either side of her. Brianna turned to go back to her room.

A hand on her shoulder halted her in her tracks. "Hello. I couldn't help but notice you're crying. Would you like to talk about it?"

Brianna refused to lift her eyes at the woman's kind words. How could she explain that she was unloved? She quietly shook her head.

"Sometimes it helps to talk about these things," the young woman urged. "I'm willing to listen, if you'd like to talk to someone."

"Thank you." Brianna lifted her head, looked into her eyes, and the woman let out a loud gasp.

"Elisabeth?" The woman's face shown astonishment.

Brianna's hands began to shake. Tears suddenly pricked her eyes. "You...you know me?" *Could it be?*

"*Ach,* of course I know you! Surely you haven't forgotten me, Lis. We've known each other our whole lives," the young woman asserted. "When you left for *Rumspringa* we didn't know if you'd ever come back. Why are you here in the hospital?"

"Do you mean to tell me I have a family?" Brianna still couldn't believe it. Dare she hope?

The young woman laughed. "Of course you have family, a pretty large one, in fact. Are you all right?"

"No." Brianna's eyes shined. "I...I had an accident. I can't remember anything from my life before."

"So, you really don't know who I am?" The woman's face showed concern.

Brianna shook her head sadly. "I'm afraid I don't even know who *I* am."

"You are Elisabeth Schrock from Paradise, Pennsylvania. I'm Rachel Brenneman, your neighbor. I'm here in New York to help my aunt Emma with her *kinner* and the new *boppli.* She just had a babe, would ya like to see him?" Rachel asked.

Brianna nodded and allowed Rachel to lead her back to the nursery window.

"See the one closest to the window in the blue crocheted cap? That's little Abe. He was named after his father who goes by Abraham. He is a nice *boppli, jah?* " Rachel's eyes glistened with pride.

"Yes, he's very cute." Brianna smiled. "Rachel, will you please help me get back home?"

"*Ach, jah.* Of course. Your *mamm* and *dat* will be ever so happy to see ya."

"They will?" Brianna asked excitedly.

"*Jah*, and poor Luke too." Rachel shook her head.

"Luke?" Brianna wondered who he was, a brother maybe.

"Luke's been pining for you somethin' awful since you left. Everyone in our district felt sorry for him. Rumor was he was gonna ask you to marry him after you both got baptized into the church," Rachel said matter-of-factly.

Brianna's eyes widened in disbelief. *I have a boyfriend?* Suddenly she noticed Rachel's attire. "Why do you dress that way?"

Rachel shook her head. "You really have forgotten everything. You have forgotten your Amish roots?"

"I'm afraid so." Brianna shrugged. "I guess I'll have to learn everything again."

"That's all right. The important thing is that you're here and you want to go home!" Rachel smiled. "I can't wait to see the look on your *mamm*'s face when she sees you again. I will talk to Aunt Emma to see if we can hire a driver to take us home."

"I have to check with the nurses. They said I was nearly done with my treatment. I..." Brianna broke down in tears again. She stood there in the hallway sobbing and allowed Rachel to pull her into a hug. "I'm sorry; it's just that I had no idea where I would go. I couldn't remember anything. I was all alone. I thought nobody loved me."

"Shh…everything will be just fine now, Elisabeth. And you have a whole community full of people who love you," Rachel asserted again.

"What's that ya got there?" Rachel moved closer on the seat and leaned over toward Brianna.

Brianna protectively covered the words she had written. "It's just my journal. The doctor suggested I keep a daily journal, so I'm writing about everything that has happened in my life since the accident." Brianna closed her journal, deciding to take a break from writing for a while. She glanced out the window and noticed the changing scenery. Gone were the looming skyscrapers of the city. They were replaced with beautiful countryside and trees galore. Pennsylvania was indeed beautiful.

"It's *schee, jah?*" Rachel noted.

"*Schee?*" Brianna cocked her head.

"I see you've forgotten your *Dietsch. Schee* means pretty," Rachel explained.

"Yes, it is *schnee*," Brianna agreed.

Rachel responded by laughing out loud.

"What? Did I say something wrong?" Brianna's confused expression caused Rachel to laugh all the more.

"I'm sorry, Elisabeth. It's just that you said *schnee*. *Schnee* means snow."

Brianna giggled then too. "I'm going to be in trouble when we get there and everyone tries to speak to me in Pennsylvania Dutch, aren't I?"

"That's okay. I'll be sure to teach you a few more words before we get there. How does that sound?" Rachel offered.

"That sounds wonderful."

"*Wunderbaar,*" Rachel corrected.

"*Wunderbaar* is wonderful. I think it would be *wunderbaar* if we could make some flash cards." Brianna smiled.

"I'll do that," Rachel said. "Why don't you go ahead and write in your journal. I'm sure you have a lot to say."

"I think I will," Brianna agreed. She flipped through the pages of her journal and read through the last few entries.

July 25 – Today was the best day of my entire life! Well, of the life I can remember anyway. I met someone today that knows who I am. Her name is Rachel and she is my neighbor. Isn't it a coincidence that we would meet in a hospital? I told Rachel that and she said that it could only be God's divine providence. I don't know much about God, but I think she's right. I guess I used to go to church all the time and pray and read the Bible. I must have been close to God. There's so much I wish I could remember.

By the way, in case I ever forget, my name is Elisabeth Schrock and I live in Paradise, Pennsylvania.

July 26 – The nurses told me I can go home tomorrow. Home! Just yesterday I had no home that I knew of. I can't express the joy that fills my heart right now. I wonder what my mom and dad are like. Or my brothers and sisters. Or Luke. I can't believe that I have a boyfriend at home waiting for me! I hope he's cute. Rachel said that he's very attractive. She described him to me and he does sound handsome. I'm a little apprehensive about meeting him though. Although he has known me my whole life, he will be a total stranger to me. What will he expect from me? I guess I will find out soon because Rachel found a driver for us and at this time tomorrow I will be home. I'm excited and scared to death all at the same time. Rachel says I should pray to help calm my nerves, so I think I will do that now.

July 27 – Today Rachel and I are traveling home. I am dressed Amish now. Rachel was kind enough to loan me some of her clothes. She said that once I get home I can wear the ones I left in my room when I left two years ago. I hope they are still there because Rachel said that if they aren't then I could just sew up some new ones. But there is one problem. I don't think I can remember how to sew. So many things I'll have to learn again. Oh well.

Right now we are riding in what Rachel calls an 'Englischer' car. We will be in Pennsylvania shortly and I can't wait to see what my home state looks like. What will my house look like? My parents? I guess I will find out in just a few hours...

FIVE

*D*riving through the traffic in New York City still grated on Elisabeth's nerves even after having her license for over a year and a half. She should have learned to drive when she was sixteen back in Pennsylvania when Luke urged her to. He said she should know how to drive just in case there was ever an emergency, but she was much too scared at the time. Driving had come naturally for Luke, it seemed. When he began his *Rumspringa* at sixteen, she was just fourteen. But Luke, even with his eagerness to drive, never really chafed against the rules the way she had. He was Amish through and through.

More and more, she realized that she didn't miss the Amish life as much as she thought she would. She had become used to all the modern *Englisch* conveniences and she enjoyed them. Sometimes she felt guilty about sitting down to watch television when the dishes had yet to be washed. Her *mamm* never would have approved. *I wonder what Mamm would think if she came to visit.* She would be shocked, to say the least.

Yet somehow Elisabeth felt like she wasn't displeasing God. At least not in the way she was living. She still went to church on Sunday and read her Bible and prayed. Her clothing was different, but not necessarily immodest. She didn't wear tight jeans or revealing tops like a lot of *Englischers* did.

The only things she missed were her family and close community. To her surprise, she didn't even miss Luke all that much. Of course, with Carson around, how could she? Carson was every bit as sweet as Luke was and every bit as good-looking too. Yet he was *Englisch*. A more suitable mate than Luke would have been for that reason alone.

Today, Carson was taking her to see the Statue of Liberty. He couldn't believe she'd been in New York for two years and had never seen the monument. Since Carson's place was closer, she agreed to meet him at his house and then he would drive from there. Shivers of excitement ran up her spine as she thought about spending the whole day with him.

This was the first time she'd ever been to his house. Carson assured her that the GPS on her Smartphone would get her there with no problems. He said he lived in a gated community and that she'd have to punch in a password to get through the gate. When she entered the suburb, she immediately realized that a higher class of people resided there. Her jaw hung open as she passed mansion after mansion. The house her parents owned in Pennsylvania was large, but these homes were fancy. Some had beautiful fountains in the front yard. Others boasted topiaries or statues. She couldn't believe the extravagance.

When she finally reached Carson's house, she was relieved to see that it wasn't as fancy as some of the other homes had been. She was nervous enough about meeting his parents. However, the house was still very nice. She parked her compact car in front of his house and he rushed to open her door for her. *Such a gentleman.* Carson said he still lived with his parents, but was ready to purchase a home of his own. He cautioned her beforehand that his parents might act a little strange around her because she looked so much like Brianna. She remembered hearing others in the past say that she looked like another girl, or that they'd seen her twin. Now she wondered if it was Carson's Brianna they spoke of. Or perhaps she just had a familiar face.

Carson held his breath as he and Elisabeth walked into his parents' home. He'd warned his parents that she looked a lot like Brianna, so he hoped they would treat her kindly and not overreact. Not that they would ever be rude to her to her face. For some reason, it seemed his parents never approved of Brianna. It was probably because they felt she was conceited and not as domesticated as they had hoped for in his choice of a mate. He felt confident that they would be pleasantly surprised with Elisabeth. Although she looked like Brianna, the two were like night and day.

Carson led Elisabeth into the great room where his parents sat reading. "Mom, Dad, I'd like you to meet my girlfriend, Elisabeth Schrock." Carson smiled broadly, grasping Elisabeth's hand.

Mrs. Welch let out a small gasp as she looked up from her novel, but quickly regained her composure. "It's nice to meet you, Elisabeth." She shook her hand.

Likewise, Mr. Welch held out his hand and smiled kindly. "Carson says this will be your first time visiting the Statue of Liberty."

Elisabeth's eyes shone brightly. "Yes, it is. I'm excited to see it. I heard you can climb the stairs all the way up the crown. I can't wait to look out over the harbor from way up high."

Carson smiled affectionately at Elisabeth, wanting to kiss her. She was so cute with her innocence and enthusiasm. He hoped his parents would see her for the gem he knew she was.

"Carson tells us you come from an Amish family," his mother commented.

"Yes, my family lives in Paradise, Pennsylvania. I left about two and half years ago," she stated.

"Don't the Amish only attend school until the eighth grade?" Carson cringed as his mother asked the demeaning question. She'd always felt that a good education was necessary to make it in the world.

"Yes, that is true. The Amish feel that an eighth grade education is sufficient for their way of life and I agree. After a scholar graduates, they usually learn the vocation that they will be working in for the rest of their life. For the girls, it's learning to do all of the tasks necessary to be a good wife and homemaker. And for the boys, they usually learn to farm, build houses, or follow in whichever trade their father works."

"That's interesting. What did you learn after you finished school?" Carson was surprised and relieved that his mother sounded truly interested.

"Just the usual things, I guess. Let's see, there's cooking, baking, canning, sewing, quilting, laundering..." as Elisabeth continued, Carson lost count, "and then, gardening, keeping house, and caring for children." She shrugged as if it was no big deal. "But when I left, my friend Mattie suggested that I study for my GED. I passed the test about two years ago, and then I was able to find an office job at Family Dental."

"I've always wanted to learn how to make a loaf of bread. My grandmother used to bake when I was little, but she passed away before I could learn." Carson couldn't believe how much his mother was latching on to Elisabeth. And he'd never seen her be sentimental.

"I would be happy to show you, if you'd like," Elisabeth offered.

Carson's father spoke up then, smiling broadly, "Carson, I think you've found a keeper."

"I agree, Dad." Carson winked at Elisabeth. "We'd love to visit more, but Elisabeth and I should get going."

"Oh, do you have to leave so soon?" his mother protested.

"I'm afraid so, Mom," Carson said.

"Why don't you bring her over for supper sometime this week? That way, we can get better acquainted." His mother looked fondly at Elisabeth.

"I would like that," Elisabeth said, flashing her beautiful smile in his direction once again.

As Carson and Elisabeth left his parents' house, he couldn't remember a time in his life when he'd been more content. Finally, he'd met a girl that his parents approved of. And it seemed they adored her just as much as he did. He smiled and patted his shirt pocket to be sure it still held its precious contents. Carson wanted this day to be absolutely perfect, and so far he was not disappointed.

SIX

As the vehicle traveled up the lane to the Schrock residence, Brianna gasped with excitement and trepidation. Home at last! Nothing looked familiar but, of course, she hadn't expected it to. She drank in the beautiful sights. Rolling green hills that seemed to stretch for miles. Large stalks of corn ready to be harvested, all neatly divided into perfectly symmetrical rows. A large white farm house with green shutters and a sprawling porch. An even larger red barn with white trim stood next to a stately concrete silo. *So this was home.* A wonderful warm sensation flooded her soul and she sent up a quick prayer of thanks to a God she had been talking to more and more lately, it seemed.

Tears filled Brianna's eyes as she watched the members of her presumed family stream out the back door of the house. As soon as the car door flew open, a woman in her forties wrapped loving arms around Brianna, tears freely flowing from her eyes. "*Dochder,* oh how I've missed you so! You're here to stay now, *jah*?"

Although Brianna didn't understand much Pennsylvania Dutch, she knew that this was her mother and that she wanted her to stay. *She wants me!* "Yes, Mother. I want to stay." Brianna smiled broadly.

Rachel then spoke up, "Remember that I told you about Elisabeth's accident. You'll have to reintroduce yourselves to her because she doesn't remember who you are. In actuality, for Elisabeth, it's like she's meeting you for the first time."

"I guess that does have its advantages," Jacob spoke up, "she won't remember all the times I got her into trouble." He laughed and held out his hand. "Hello *schweschder*, I'm your favorite brother, Jacob."

Brianna enjoyed his playful spirit and didn't doubt that they had probably gotten along well in the past. "Hello, brother. Nice to meet you...again."

Jacob pointed to his siblings. "This is Mary, and she is five. Martha here is seven. Paul is ten. Tabitha is twelve. James is thirteen. Michael is sixteen. And I am eighteen."

A man with a long brownish-gray beard stepped forward and patted her shoulder somewhat hesitantly. "*Gut* to see you, Elisabeth."

"You are my father, right?" Brianna noticed a slight misting of his eyes after she said the words and he nodded affirmatively. "It is *gut* to see you too, Dad."

"Let us go inside now. Supper is almost ready. Jacob, show your sister to her room so she can put her things away and wash for dinner," *Mamm* Schrock dictated. "Rachel, you are welcome to stay for supper."

Rachel briefly locked eyes with Jacob, and then looked away. "I should probably get home soon. *Mamm* is expecting me. Elisabeth, I will come by and see you tomorrow." Rachel leaned over to embrace Brianna. "Study your flashcards," she whispered in her ear.

"Thank you for everything, Rachel." Brianna sincerely meant every word. She waved to her friend, and then followed Jacob inside her new home.

Elisabeth huffed as she climbed the final steps up to the crown of the Statue of Liberty. She glanced at Carson, who seemed a little winded himself, and then laughed. "For an Amish girl who's worked hard physically for most of her life, you'd think I could handle a few stairs with no problem."

"A few stairs?" Carson asked incredulously. "I think I'd call that a little more than a few. One hundred fifty-four steps, to be exact."

"Shall we take a look at the view?" Elisabeth smiled and Carson took her hand and led her to the lookout.

"It's beautiful, isn't it?" he stated unnecessarily.

"Oh wow! This is amazing. I can see everything from up here." She glanced over at Carson to see him looking at the view as well. "Look at the skyscrapers. We're as tall as they are."

"That's Manhattan right there." Carson pointed out. "And there's the Brooklyn Bridge."

"*Ach*, the people look like ants all the way down there." Elisabeth gasped. She'd never seen such a sight.

"So, do you like it?" Carson smiled, his arm draped around her shoulders.

"Yes, it's magnificent!" She gazed into his sparkling eyes.

Carson lowered his voice. "You know, I think you're pretty magnificent." He lowered his head and pressed his lips to hers. While she was distracted, he pulled out a surprise from his shirt pocket.

Elisabeth gasped when she saw the beautiful diamond ring.

"Elisabeth, will you marry me?" Carson's gaze was intense, and when she nodded, he happily slipped the ring onto her finger and sealed their engagement with another sweet kiss.

Luke stared out at an open field through the kitchen window of his house. A sultry breeze wafted to his nostrils bringing with it the faint scent of fresh baked bread from his folks' place. There would have been bread baking in *this* house if Elisabeth hadn't gone. Frustration mounted as he thought about all he'd lost when Elisabeth left. Luke couldn't help the feelings of unforgiveness and bitterness that now resided in his heart. How could someone carry on a relationship for two years and then just walk away without even saying goodbye?

He'd begun building this house, that was intended to be a home for him and Elisabeth, before she had left. He'd completed construction on it last fall. It was to be the place where they would build their lives together, share their hopes and dreams, and raise a family who would continue their Plain traditions and faith in God.

But perhaps God had other plans. That sure seemed to be the case as he stood in the large vacant dwelling. Alone. Was he destined to a life of bachelordom?

A knock at the back door startled him. Rachel Brenneman's younger brother stood on the porch.

"Rachel wanted me to give you a message," the boy said slowly, staring at his bangs as if trying to remember her exact words.

Luke waited patiently, slowly tapping his fingers against his thigh.

"Oh yeah. She said, 'Go tell Luke that Elisabeth is home.' I think that was it."

Luke blinked his eyes a few times, absorbing the words. "Elisabeth Schrock? She's home? Are you sure?"

"That's what my sister said to tell you. Came home just a little while ago all excited. Told *Mamm* she found her in New York City when she helped Aunt Emma with her *boppli*. Rachel don't lie none, so I reckon it's true." He stared up at Luke through his blond locks as though waiting to be dismissed.

"All right, *denki*." Luke patted the boy's shoulder. The boy turned on his heel and raced off through the back field.

Dare he hope? Could it possibly be true?

What he felt like doing was hollering a big 'Whoop!' He wanted to race over to Elisabeth's place, take her into his arms, and never let her go again.

But no, he scowled, strengthening his resolve. How could he just go over there and take her back as though had ever happened, as though she hadn't done anything wrong? Surely that's what she'd expect. He wasn't about to give her that satisfaction. No. He would go see her and find out if she was remorseful at all. If he saw that she was contrite, then, and only then would he take her back.

Nevertheless, his heart soared at the thought of seeing his precious Beth again.

Although the day had been exciting, Brianna was now exhausted and ready for bed. Her brothers and sisters had peppered her with questions after supper, most of which she could not answer. She wondered how many times she would have to tell the story of the accident and how Rachel found her in the hospital. She loved telling the latter, but her time in the hospital was shrouded with the pain of loneliness she'd felt. But thankfully, that was all behind her now. Today would start a new chapter in her life.

Brianna was almost asleep when she heard a noise outside. She tried to ignore it, but the noise persisted so she dragged herself out of bed to look out the window. When she opened the curtain, she saw a small rock hit the glass pane. She looked to the ground outside and was frightened when she saw a man with a flashlight. She immediately stepped back from the window. *Oh no, someone is trying to break into the house!* She couldn't believe this was happening on her first night back. She'd need to alert the family to keep everyone safe from harm.

"AAH!! Somebody help!" she screamed at the top of her lungs.

Within a minute, her entire family was standing in her doorway. *"Was iss letz,* Elisabeth?" her father asked, wide-eyed.

She stared back at him in confusion.

"He asked what is wrong," Jacob clarified.

Brianna began trembling, pointing toward the window. "There...there was a man standing outside on the lawn! He was throwing rocks at the window. I think he was trying to break into the house, but my screaming scared him off."

Jacob looked at his father with a smile and they both roared with laughter. Brianna's confused look only made things worse and the others joined in as well, including *Mamm.*

"I don't understand." Brianna looked from one to the other.

Jacob took a few deep breaths to keep from cracking up more as he explained, "You just scared off your beau. That was most likely Luke coming to see you!" He couldn't help but burst into laughter again.

Brianna's hands flew to her cheeks, which immediately reddened. "Oh. I...I didn't know."

"I'll explain how Amish courtship works in the morning." *Mamm* smiled, patting Brianna's arm. "Now, it's time for everyone to get to bed." She looked at all of the children and they obeyed immediately.

Before Jacob left, he turned to Brianna. "I love having you home, Elisabeth. I can tell we're going to have a lot of fun with you around again."

Brianna was left alone with her thoughts. *I guess I have a lot to learn about being Amish. I hope Luke understands.* She yawned, snuggled under her quilt, and fell into a peaceful night of sleep.

SEVEN

*K*nock. *Knock. Knock.* Brianna groaned and pulled the covers over her head, attempting to block out the noise. *Knock. Knock. Knock.* She turned over in her bed, this time burying her face in the pillow. *I wish those nurses would go away. Don't they know that the patients need their sleep?*

"Elisabeth, it's time to get up now," she heard a male voice call from the door.

Brianna's eyes immediately flew open. Understanding swiftly dawned on her. *I'm home. That was my brother.* "Uh, okay. I'll get dressed and be downstairs in just a little bit."

"You better hurry," Jacob said in a teasing sing-song voice. "I'm sure somebody will be over to see you soon."

"Who?" She poked her head through the door, not caring that her hair stuck up in places and it hadn't been brushed yet.

"Remember the boogie man from last night?" He chuckled.

"My...my..."

"*Jah*, your beau. Luke. He's already been over once this morning and I told him you were being lazy." He smiled.

Brianna gasped. "You did not!"

"No, I didn't. But I did say you were still sleeping, so he might have thought it just the same." He laughed.

Unexpectedly, Brianna grabbed a pillow from her bed and bopped Jacob on the head with it. Jacob then caught the pillow and flung it back at her.

"You don't have time to play right now, *schweschder*. Don't forget *Mamm* still has to teach you about Amish courtship. And she'd better make it quick by the look of it, because Luke is awfully eager to see you." Jacob knew he shouldn't tease, but he was just having too much fun seeing his sister in such a state. Jacob shook his head and pulled the door to close it.

"Jacob, wait!" Brianna called desperately. "What does he want?"

"Who, Luke?" he asked, scratching his head. She nodded back. "My guess is he'll want to take you behind the barn and do some smooching. Then after that, he'll want to take your *kapp* off so he can run his fingers through your –"

"Jacob!" a gruff voice called from behind him, which she recognized as their father's. "Don't you have chores to tend to?"

Brianna heard Jacob's hurried steps clomping down the stairs. Her father knocked on the door, but didn't open it. Instead, he mumbled through the door, "Pay no mind to your brother's foolishness."

"Yes, Father. Please tell Mother I will be down in just a bit," Brianna said.

"All right, we will see you downstairs shortly." Brianna then heard her father's footsteps descend the stairs as well.

Brianna brushed her hair with haste and tried her best to pin it up in a bun the way Rachel had yesterday. Several strands of hair fell down around her face and neck. She placed her *kapp* on her head and secured it with a pin, and then reached into her closet to find one of her old dresses. She picked out a plain blue dress and pinned on her black apron, glad that she apparently hadn't gained any weight since she left two and a half years ago. She brushed her teeth and rushed downstairs to start her day, excited to learn all about the life she had lived for most of her twenty years.

The moment she arrived in the kitchen, she knew she'd done something wrong. Her mother shook her head and clucked her tongue, but pulled her into an embrace just the same. "I still can't believe that *mei dochder* has come home. Although, I can tell you will need much training before you can become a *gut fraa* for Luke Beiler."

Brianna's cheeks reddened once again. She remembered from her flash cards that *fraa* meant wife in this context.

"First, come sit and I will fix your hair." As her mother unwound the bun Brianna had secured just moments before, she explained why Luke had come to her window last night. "Normally, our young people court in secret. It is the Amish way. The young folks attend singings on Sunday nights. They don't just sing, though. Sometimes, they will play games like volleyball or baseball. Usually a nice snack is served and the boys and girls talk amongst themselves. But it's usually girls with girls and boys with boys, otherwise it is not proper. When the time winds down, that is when a boy will ask a girl if he may take her home in his buggy. If they are both agreeable after the first ride, they may begin a courtship that leads to marriage."

Brianna's mind swam with questions as anxiety began to build. "But, how long am I allowed to stay out on Sunday nights? What should I do if Luke comes to my window at night again? What do the boys and girls do when they ride home in the buggy? What if I go to the singing and nobody asks me to ride home? I don't know if I can find my way back home by myself. I'm...I'm kind of scared to go. I don't really know anyone except my brothers and sisters and Rachel. And –"

"*Ach*, slow down, *mei maedel*. Too much worry is not *gut*. Jacob will go to the singing with you. He will be sure that you have a ride home. Your friends will be happy to see you. Trust in *Der Herr*. He will be with you," her mother assured her, and then securely fastened her prayer *kapp* once again.

Brianna took a deep breath, allowing herself to relax. "*Denki, Mamm*," Brianna practiced her Pennsylvania Dutch.

"Now, you must eat something. You are hungry, *jah*?" *Mamm* Schrock asked, while pulling out some fresh bread with butter and jam. Brianna nodded, and *Mamm* fluttered about the kitchen while she ate.

"Where is everybody?"

"Martha, Paul, Tabitha, and James are in school. Mary is outside helping Michael and Joseph with chores. Your *vatter* is out in the field," *Mamm* informed her. "Everyone has their chores and helps out, so the home runs smoothly."

"What is my chore?" she wondered aloud.

"*Ach*, before you left you would help me bake the bread and desserts every day. We would do the wash together on Mondays. You would help with mending and teaching the smaller ones. You always helped with dishes after every meal. And on Wednesdays and Fridays you would cook supper."

Brianna watched as *Mamm*'s eyes teared up. "What is it, *Mamm*?" She stood from the table and edged closer to *Mamm* Schrock, attempting to offer comfort.

"I've just missed you so. When you left, my heart broke in two. I didn't know if I would ever see the daughter I first gave birth to." She quickly brushed away the unbidden tears.

"I'm sorry, Mom. I'm sorry for leaving. I don't know what I was thinking." And that was the truth, she realized. She patted *Mamm*'s hand and turned when she heard footsteps.

The back door swung open and in walked Jacob, accompanied by a young man. An attractive one, at that. Brianna quickly turned toward the sink, not wanting to seem too eager to meet Jacob's visitor.

"*Ach*, I must go outside to check on the *kinner* now. Jacob, you will help me," *Mamm* dictated.

"*Jah, Mamm*," Jacob agreed. "Luke, do you mind waiting for me here? I'll be back shortly."

Brianna turned to see Jacob give her a wink, and then he sauntered out the door with an enormous grin. Brianna stood near the sink in silence, unsure of what she should say to the handsome stranger.

"Hullo, Elisabeth." Luke stood by the door holding his hat in his hands, seemingly just as nervous as she was. "I…I've missed you."

Brianna allowed her eyes to wander up to his face. Immediately, she noticed his eyes. They were as blue as the beautiful sun-filled sky after a rainy day. His golden hair trimmed his face in the style that most Amish men wore. The blue shirt he wore under his black suspenders accentuated his eyes, along with his broad shoulders and toned arms. As far as Brianna was concerned, this man standing in her kitchen – her beau – was as close to perfection as one could possibly get.

"Jacob told me about the accident," he stated, attempting to make conversation.

"What did he say?" she finally found her voice, trying not to stare.

Luke took a few steps closer, and then paused. "He told me that Rachel saw you in the hospital and you didn't know who you were. He also said you don't remember anything from the past." His eyes begged for an invitation to come near.

"Would…would you like to sit down?" She gestured toward the table.

"Jah, denki." He moved to the table and sat on the bench where her brothers had sat for the evening meal.

Brianna took the bench opposite him, hesitant to look into his eyes. At least she was sitting now and no longer had to fear her knees would buckle. She spoke in a near whisper, "Did Jacob tell you that I have a brain injury? I have something called Retrograde Amnesia. I'm able to remember the things that have happened after I woke up from my coma, but my mind has forgotten everything from before. I didn't remember my name or who my family was or where I came from. And I'm sorry, Luke. But I…I can't remember you either," as she said the words, tears spilled over her eyelashes and down her cheeks. Her heart was engulfed by loneliness, pain, and guilt.

In one fluid movement, Luke was by her side. He drew her head to his chest and held her tight while she sobbed. "Shh…it's all right, Beth. None of that matters now. You're home. You're here and that's all that matters to me." His rugged scent and strong arms provided the viable comfort she'd been craving.

When Brianna caught her breath, she spoke again, "I don't understand. Why did I leave here? Why would anyone ever want to leave?"

"I can't answer that, Elisabeth. Because I don't know." He released her, and she realized she was saddened by the action. "But I do know that I still love you."

Brianna peered up at him and smiled, brushing away the tears. "I'm sure I don't deserve you. I…I left."

Pain still stabbed at Luke's heart when he remembered how he'd felt the day she left, but he chose to let it go. His earlier resolve disappeared. His anger quickly melted away, now replaced with forgiveness and compassion. "Don't say that, *Lieb*. The past is forgiven. We're together now. And I'm hoping that this time you'll stay and be my sweetheart…and marry me."

She looked into Luke's pleading blue eyes and saw love. Brianna's heart melted like candle wax under a hot flame.

"I don't want to leave anymore. I want to stay here…with you. But…" she hesitated, then continued, "I am not ready to get married just yet. I know that I was your girlfriend, your *aldi* before. To me, though, you still feel like a stranger. I want to get to know you and it might take some time. I hope you understand."

Luke grasped her hand, and held her gaze. "Take all the time you need, Beth. But it would make me really happy if we could marry this fall. I want to show you the place I built for us. We have fifty acres of land that we can farm and there're plenty of rooms in the house for lots of *bopplin*." His cheeks immediately reddened when he realized he'd gotten carried away in his excitement.

Brianna just smiled as her cheeks darkened too. "I would love to see the place."

"I'd love to see the place too!" Jacob boomed as he clambered through the doorway.

Luke abruptly put proper distance between himself and Brianna. He stood up from the table and placed his hat on his head. "I best be goin' now. You're comin' to the youth gathering this Saturday, right?" Luke seemed as if he asked them both and Brianna looked to Jacob for confirmation.

"We might just do that. But I think I'm taking Sarah Anne home so you'll have to find your own ride, *Schweschder.*" Brianna's face heated again. Her brother couldn't have been more insinuating…or embarrassing.

"No need to worry about that." Luke tipped his hat and smiled before exiting the house. Brianna thought for sure her heart would sprout wings and fly right out of her chest. Could there ever be anyone sweeter than the man who had just walked out the door?

Luke practically skipped home, unable to keep from grinning. He combed his mind, arriving at the conclusion that he'd never been happier. *Beth is home!* Oh, but she'd never been so beautiful and sweet. Although he thought it odd that she couldn't remember anything, apparently not even her *Dietsch* by the way she spoke. But none of that mattered. Elisabeth was here and he'd even held her in his arms! Surely her scent would linger with him throughout the day and fill his dreams this night. Saturday couldn't come quickly enough.

He wasn't sure what all she'd gone through out in the world, but was certain the accident and her subsequent amnesia had been beneficial. She had never seemed so vulnerable, so humble. Suddenly he'd been overcome with an overwhelming desire to love, comfort, and protect her. And the best way he could think to do that was by taking her as his bride. But first, he'd have to prove himself. Prove that he was worthy of her love.

EIGHT

Elisabeth's gaze moved over the many empty boxes in her apartment. She couldn't believe that her friend Mattie was getting married. How different their lives had turned out from what they'd had planned as little girls. Back then they were certain they'd be married to good, hardworking Amish men. They'd even role played sometimes. One of them would be the Amishman coming in from the fields after a hard day's work, and the other would be the wife putting supper on the table and tending to the *bopplin*. Sometimes she'd even make her younger brother Jacob pretend that he was the Amishman.

She smiled at the fond memory, and then shook her head at the absurdity of it all. Now she was engaged to a gorgeous, wealthy *Englischer* who made his living by trading on the stock market. The two images were complete polar opposites. Even so, she was still looking forward to a houseful of children.

Mattie spoke up, pulling her out of her reverie, "What was that smile for?" She folded another one of her towels and placed it into a box.

"I was just thinking of when we were *kinner*. Do you remember when we would pretend we were getting married?" She smiled at her childhood friend.

Mattie's eyes lit up. "Yes, I do. Poor Jacob, we always made him do our bidding." She laughed.

"I remember when you had a crush on Jake Yoder and you insisted Jacob pretend that he was him. But Jacob didn't want to because he secretly had a crush on you."

"No, he didn't!" Mattie protested.

"Yes, he did." Elisabeth shook her head adamantly. "That's why he kissed you after the 'ceremony'!"

Mattie laughed. "I remember that! I was so mad at him." She shook her head. "And the whole time he was crushin' on me. Oh, that's so sweet."

Elisabeth laughed, a bittersweet moment to be sure.

"And you liked Luke Beiler, even back then."

"I think most of my fascination with Luke was infatuation and his good looks." Elisabeth decided.

"I don't know. I think it was more than that. All I remember is once Luke noticed you were alive, he was head over heels. No one could even hold a candle next to you in his mind's eye." Mattie reminisced. "How did you break it off with him? What did he say when you left?"

Elisabeth suddenly turned more serious. "I couldn't tell him. I knew if I had to face him, then he'd talk me into staying. I couldn't do it. So I just left a note."

Mattie cringed. "Oh, Lis. You can't be serious! I bet poor Luke is dying of a broken heart even as we speak."

"Don't say that. I feel bad, I really do. I guess I took the coward's way out." Elisabeth shrugged.

"Well, I guess it's all in God's hands anyway. He has a way of making things turn out," Mattie asserted.

"Yes, He does. Doesn't He? Thank you for reminding me of that, Mattie." She gave her friend a hug. "Sometimes it's hard not to second guess the choices I've made."

"I know what you mean. When life brings changes, I think we tend to do that more." Mattie wiped away a tear. "I miss the old life sometimes, but I know this is God's will for me. And God's will is always best, whether we realize it at the time or not."

"I'm glad you're marrying Richard. He's a fine Christian man and I know he will love you," Lis added.

"Me, too." Mattie took a deep breath. "So when does your new roommate move in?"

"In two weeks. I guess that'll be about the time you and Richard are cruising the Caribbean." Elisabeth couldn't help the envy that crept up.

"I can't wait!" Mattie shrieked. "Have you and Carson discussed a honeymoon yet?"

"No, but I think I'd like to visit the Hawaiian Islands. Or maybe Fiji," Elisabeth said dreamy-eyed.

"This is crazy, you know! Two Plain little country girls living in New York City and marrying two fancy *Englischers.*" Mattie laughed.

"Yes, well, neither of us will be marrying anyone if we don't stop talking and get these boxes packed." Elisabeth looked at the clock and realized half of the day had flown by. "And I have a date with my fancy *Englischer* tonight. We're having dinner at his folks' house."

Rachel made the short trek over to the Schrocks' home to see how Elisabeth was faring. Since she lived just over on the other side of the hill, she'd always cut through the Schrocks' pasture. One time her mother had scolded her for tearing her dress on the fence post and she had since learned to be more cautious.

When she entered the neighbors' property, she spotted Jacob out riding one of their painted mares. She enjoyed riding horses as well. Sometimes, when they were younger, she and Jacob would ride together. That had come to an abrupt stop when her mother had found out about it. She insisted it wasn't proper for a *maedel* to ride astride a horse – especially accompanied by a young man. But it wasn't before Rachel's heart was stolen away. She thought maybe Jacob had feelings for her too, but after they stopped riding together he seemed to distance himself from her. She always wondered why.

Jacob rode up to her with a smile and tipped his hat. "Would you like a lift?" His eyes sparkled.

Oh, how she wished she could say yes. "*Ach*, I better not. *Mamm* doesn't think it's proper."

"*Jah*, sure, your *mamm*," he said with a hint of sarcasm, rolling his eyes. "Whatever you say, Rachel." And with a huff, he rode off in the opposite direction.

Rachel swallowed the lump in her throat. Jacob didn't have to be rude just because she wasn't allowed to ride with him. Maybe she should quit holding out for Jacob and ride home with Jake Yoder at the next singing. It was obvious Jacob had no interest in her, so she may as well. Jacob hadn't asked her to go riding in his buggy once, but she'd already had two offers from Jake. Although she didn't care for him in a special way, surely it wouldn't hurt to be taken home by a good-looking young man.

"Oh no! Not again!" Rachel heard Brianna's voice cry from inside the house. Rachel quickly entered the back door and coughed when she was engulfed in a billow of smoke. She waved the smoke away from her eyes in an attempt to see her way to the stove.

"Elisabeth, *was iss letz?*" She hurried over to the oven, grabbed a potholder, and pulled out what looked like a burnt blackberry pie.

"*Mamm* went into town and I wanted to surprise her by having dessert made when she returned home," Brianna whined.

"She'll be surprised all right," Rachel said, turning the oven off before it caught fire. "You should have asked me to come over and help you."

"I'm afraid I must've left the strawberry pie in longer than it was supposed to be." She sighed.

Rachel's eyes widened. "*Those* are strawberries?" She tried to hold it in, but couldn't help it when a burst of laughter escaped her lips.

"How will I ever be able to get married if I can't bake?" Brianna said miserably.

"Why don't you come over to my house a couple of times a week and I can teach you?" Rachel offered.

"Really, Rachel? You would do that for me?" She couldn't get over her friend's kind offer.

"Of course I would. Let's start tomorrow, if it suits you."

"Tomorrow would be *wunderbaar!*" Brianna exclaimed.

NINE

Elisabeth couldn't get over how much she enjoyed the company of Carson's family. His parents had invited their other son Clark and his wife over for dinner as well. Clark reminded Elisabeth of her own brother, Jacob, whom she often missed. His wife Evan seemed to be really kind too, but she couldn't help noticing the awkward glances she received every now and then. She was beginning to wish she and Brianna didn't look so much alike.

She took another bite of the delicious vegan lasagna Carson's mother had prepared. She wasn't accustomed to many vegan dishes, growing up Amish and all. Her family lived mostly off of the bounty produced by the farm animals: eggs from the chickens, milk from the cows, and meat from whatever her father and brothers brought back from hunting, and of course the farm animals themselves. Carson informed Elisabeth that he was vegan strictly for health reasons. He knew the Bible taught that there was nothing spiritually wrong with eating animal products and warned against those who command abstinence from meat. Carson stood to reason that God's people could do so much more for Him if they weren't sick all the time, and to that Elisabeth had to agree.

She had already begun researching on the internet how to adapt her favorite Amish recipes into vegan ones. If she ever went back home to visit, she decided she would contact Danika Yoder. She knew the Yoders and the Kings, owners of the local health food store, ate healthier than most and figured they probably had some good recipes she could try. So far, the recipes she'd attempted had tasted okay. But she knew it would take practice to make them truly delicious.

Carson suddenly stood up from the table and cleared his throat. He took Elisabeth's hand and gazed lovingly into her eyes. "Elisabeth and I have an announcement to make. I have asked her to marry me and she has agreed," he declared with a smile.

Elisabeth glimpsed the faces around the table, but no one else seemed to be smiling. In fact, everyone appeared to be speechless.

Carson's mother gasped. "I'm sorry about our reaction, Son. It's just that it's so soon. Don't get me wrong," she said, turning to Elisabeth, "we love Elisabeth and all, but are the two of you ready to take this step?"

"Mother, if I didn't feel I was ready then I wouldn't have asked her. I love Elisabeth and I know I want to spend the rest of my life with her," Carson declared.

Carson's father spoke up, "Well, then I guess congratulations are in order. How about some nice stemware for the sparkling cider?" He turned to his wife, who nodded and then brought some fancy gold-rimmed goblets to the table. They popped open a bottle, then poured a small amount into each glass.

Carson's mother handed one to Elisabeth, who took it hesitantly. A bit confused, she decided to speak up, "I'm sorry, but I don't drink alcoholic beverages."

"Oh, neither do we, sweetheart. This is just sparkling cider. It's like juice with carbonated water added to it." She patted her hand and Elisabeth released a nervous sigh.

"Shall we propose a toast?" Carson's father stood up and asked in a formal sounding voice. Elisabeth had no idea what all this meant, but she went along with it and nodded her head like the others. "To my oldest son Carson and his fiancée Elisabeth: May you have a long, happy, and prosperous life together. And may you serve the Lord all of your days."

Elisabeth followed suit as everyone held up their glasses and gently touched them one to another, each one making a tinkling sound as they did. "Cheers!" they all said to each other, and then happily drank down the sweet fizzy beverage. Even though different, Elisabeth decided she enjoyed this strange *Englisch* custom. After all, it was vastly different than the 'publishing' that went on when an Amish couple's engagement was announced.

The dinner resumed and Carson's family bombarded the happy couple with a plethora of questions. The main one being:

"When's the big day?" Of course, Elisabeth didn't know the answer to that since she and Carson hadn't discussed a wedding date yet. But as the evening wore on and the awkwardness dissipated, Elisabeth found herself more and more excited about her upcoming wedding.

"Jacob, I'm really nervous about attending the gathering tonight," Brianna said, squeezing his arm as she sat next to him in his buggy.

Jacob laughed. "Well if you keep squeezing my arm like that, neither one of us will going to the gathering. Will you let go, please?"

"Oh, sorry. I didn't realize I was doing that." Brianna let go and scooted over a bit.

"What are you so nervous about?" Jacob asked.

"Well, I don't really know anyone. Except for maybe Rachel." She fidgeted.

"And you know Luke." He reminded her, casting a knowing smile her way.

"Yeah, well. I guess I'm kind of nervous about him too. I...I've never ridden home with anyone before," Brianna said, twisting up the side of her apron.

Jacob laughed. "You're acting like you're fourteen and this is your first singing. Elisabeth, you've gone on many buggy rides with Luke. This one will probably be no different."

"But I don't remember any of those. This is like my first gathering. I don't know what Luke will expect from me." She attempted to calm her nerves, but it seemed the closer they got to the gathering the more tense she became.

Jacob turned to her and patted her arm. "He expects you to be you. You don't have to worry that he's going to take advantage of you or anything. Luke is not that kind of person. If you decide that you don't want to go home with him, then I will take you home. Does that make you feel better?"

Brianna blew out a nervous breath, and then leaned over and kissed his cheek. "*Jah, denki,* Jacob."

"Hey, that's what little brothers are for." He reached over and playfully pulled out one of her hair pins. Brianna grabbed it back and fastened it to her bun again.

"You're going to ask Sarah to ride home with you?" She lifted an eyebrow.

"Sarah Anne Yoder, *jah.*" He shrugged as if it was no big deal.

"Why don't you ask Rachel? Aren't the two of you the same age?" Brianna suggested.

Jacob's eyebrows lifted curiously. "Why would you ask about *her*?"

"I think Rachel is really kind. And she's pretty, don't ya think?" She hinted.

"That may be the case, but Rachel has no desire to ride in *my* buggy," Jacob asserted.

"So you've already asked her before and she turned you down?"

"I didn't say that." He shook his head.

"So you like her, but you're afraid to ask her," Brianna stated, but Jacob remained conspicuously silent. "Ah ha, that's it!"

"Is not," he denied, his cheeks blushing furiously.

"Is so. How cute! My little brother has a crush on my best friend," Brianna taunted.

"You better not say anything!" he threatened.

She threatened him back, crossing her arms. "I won't, *if* you ask her home."

"You can just forget about the buggy ride I offered you earlier." He huffed.

"That's okay, I don't need it. I'm riding home with Luke," she declared smugly, and then turned up her nose.

TEN

Brianna sat next to Rachel on a bale of hay that had been moved outside the barn. They watched on the sidelines as their peers played softball. Many of her former friends and schoolmates had come to say hello, welcoming her back into the community. More and more, Brianna was feeling like part of the Amish community and it helped to ease some of her anxiety.

Luke had briefly waved at her before joining the other guys on the field. Rachel told her it was normal for the young men to act nonchalant, and necessary in order to keep courtships secret. Brianna was a bit relieved because she wasn't sure what she would say to him anyway. Her nerves were still a bit raw, and became more so as the sun descended on the horizon.

Brianna didn't ask Rachel if she had her eye on anyone because it didn't seem the proper thing to do. She was curious if Rachel had feelings for her brother, however. Hopefully, Jacob would get the chance to drive Rachel home tonight and it would be the beginning of a beautiful courtship.

Soon the games ended and young people gathered around the bonfire. Folding chairs and hay bales formed a large circle several feet from the small inferno. The boys and girls sat on opposite sides, but it seemed Luke sat where he could catch Brianna's eye. As the singing began, Brianna fell in love with the mixture of melodic voices. She felt closer to God somehow as she joined in with others in praise to her Maker.

When the singing ceased, the young folks gathered in the barn for snacks and fellowship. It was there that Luke approached Brianna and confirmed their plan for him to take her home. A nervous excitement rose up in Brianna's belly and she hoped she could calm it before Luke's buggy ride.

Rachel snatched a napkin from the snack table and placed two chocolate chip cookies in it. She felt someone next to her and looked up to see Jake Yoder nearby.

"Hello, Rachel." Jake smiled.

"Hello, Jake. Are you having a nice evening?" She tried to make polite conversation.

"*Jah*, 'tis nice. But it would be even nicer if you'll let me drive you home tonight." Jake twisted his hat nervously in his hands.

"*Jah*, all right Jake," she agreed, and then smiled at the look of surprise on his face.

"Really?" His dark eyes brightened.

"*Jah*, I would like to ride home with you." Rachel gave him a reassuring smile.

"Uh...*denki*, Rachel. I will get my buggy ready directly." He turned and walked out of the barn with a spring in his step.

Rachel went and sat down next to Brianna. They had just begun a conversation when Jacob walked up to them. "Rachel, may I speak with you, please?"

Rachel looked at Brianna who stood up. "I need to go now," Brianna said and walked outside the barn leaving them alone.

"You wanted to talk to me, Jacob?" Rachel looked into his eager eyes and hoped he wasn't about to ask her what she thought he might.

"May I take you home tonight?" He seemed a little more nervous than usual.

Finally Jacob asked her and she had to turn him down! She shook her head regretfully, not wanting to say the words. "I'm sorry, Jacob. But I –"

Rachel was abruptly cut off when he held out his hand to silence her. "Let me guess. Your *mother* won't let you go? You know what? Never mind! I only asked you because Elisabeth forced me to anyway. I knew I should have just asked Sarah Anne," he said angrily, and then stomped off.

Rachel put her hands over her face and sighed, her face red with embarrassment...and hurt...and anger. Why did Jacob's words have to cut so deep? *I can't believe this. I don't know why I ever liked Jacob Schrock in the first place!* She stood up, brushed the hay from her dress, and went to meet Jake Yoder at his buggy.

Brianna fiddled with her *kapp* string as she waited for Luke to join her in his buggy. She took a couple of deep breaths as Luke readied the horse, hoping to calm her nervousness. What would they do? Would he drive her straight home? Would they be able to find things to talk about? What if she wasn't the same girl as before? What if he got to know her and discovered he didn't like her anymore? Or worse yet, what if he tried to kiss her?

Her thoughts were interrupted when Luke hopped up into the buggy. He offered a reassuring smile. For some reason, she never realized how small the buggy seats were until now. Probably because they sat in such close proximity to one another. Or maybe this was just how Luke's buggy was made. As Luke took up the reins, their arms brushed, sending delicious shivers up her spine. He clicked his tongue to get the large beast moving.

She was sure there were many girls envious of her right now. How could they not be? Luke was certainly the finest-looking boy at the gathering tonight. She knew she was swooning over him, but felt she had no control over it. Luke had already professed his love. He had expressed his intentions of marriage. All of this just seemed too good to be true. As if she'd stepped right into a fairy tale.

"What did you think of the gathering? Did you have a *gut* time?" Luke's blue eyes shined from under his straw hat.

"Yes. I had a wonderful time, although I was a bit nervous. Still am."

Luke appreciated her honesty. The previous Elisabeth wouldn't have been so forthcoming. He reached over and clasped her hand. "*Ach*, you don't need to feel nervous with me. If I do something that makes you uncomfortable, please let me know."

He was so caring, so considerate. She just could not understand why or how she could have left him. Or her family, for that matter. Hadn't she known what she was walking away from? "I still don't understand why I left. Did you and I have an argument or something?"

"*Nee*. And as far as I know you were at peace with your family as well. I think you were just tired of being Amish. Wanted to go off and live in the big city." He sighed.

"You know, it's kinda funny. I'm frustrated with myself because I left, yet I can't remember any of it." She shook her head as if trying to jar a memory.

"*Lieb*, let's not talk about the past anymore. I've forgiven you. You must forgive yourself as well," Luke stated, stroking her hand with his large thumb. She noticed how small her hand was inside his and she felt a sense of comfort and security.

Brianna looked up and saw the pain in Luke's eyes. For the first time, she realized she must have really hurt him deeply. She determined from that moment on not to mention the past anymore. She couldn't bear seeing the hurt in his eyes and the pain etched across his lovely face, so she changed the subject. "Tell me about Him."

"Who?" Luke wore a puzzled expression.

Brianna laughed. "I guess I can't expect you to be a mind reader. God, I mean."

"Oh Beth, you really have changed." He smiled. "In a good way. What would you like to know about God?"

"Everything," she stated, oblivious to the beautiful scenery passing them by.

Luke laughed. "I'm afraid nobody knows everything about God. If we did then He wouldn't be God, *jah*?"

She nodded. "Tell me what you know."

"That might take a while." He leaned over and whispered in her ear, "You got all night?"

Maybe it was his hot breath against her cheek or the sensuous way he seemed to ask, but Brianna got the feeling he was referring to more than just talking. "I...I don't –"

Luke laughed out loud. "Relax. I'm teasing you, Beth. And just to put your mind at ease, you should know that I intend to stay pure. We won't...I mean, until our wedding night..." he said, suddenly uncomfortable.

Brianna laughed. "It's all right, Luke. I know what you mean."

Luke sighed, and then arched an eyebrow. "But you don't mind if I kiss you, do you?"

"Right now?" she squeaked, swallowing hard.

He laughed again. "Well, no. Not right now...unless you want to."

She shook her head outwardly, but inside she was nodding.

"That's what I suspected. I meant just whenever," he clarified.

"I...I think I might like that. We are getting married, right?" She blushed.

"Nothing would make me happier," he declared, and then suddenly remembered her original question before they got sidetracked. "You were asking about God."

"I was. I want to know more about Him. Since the accident...well, Rachel said I should talk to Him." She shrugged. "I did, a few times."

"Prayer is an important part in our relationship with God. Just like it is important for the two of us to communicate. If we don't talk to each other, we won't know how the other one feels," he explained. "When we do talk to each other, our relationship becomes stronger and we understand each other better."

"I see. So I can talk to God just as if he's sitting right next to me?" She seemed skeptical.

"Well, if you are a child of God, He is even closer than that."

"How do I know if I'm a child of God?"

Luke smiled. He was taken aback by her innocence. She was like a child in so many ways: so impressionable, so trusting. "Has your father read the Bible to you since you've been back?"

"*Jah*, he reads it at night after supper and in the morning too. But I have to admit there is a lot I don't understand."

"Sometimes God only reveals bits and pieces of His Word to us because we are not ready for more. Then, when we are ready He gives us more understanding." He continued, "Sometimes I will read a verse that I've read many times, but this particular time it will stand out to me and I will see something that I never saw before."

"I think I understand." She looked up as if trying to store the information in her mind.

"The Bible calls those who have received Him – who have faith in His Son Jesus Christ – His children. Have you received Jesus Christ?" Luke asked sincerely.

"What do you mean by 'receive Him'?" She cocked her head and Luke couldn't get over how sweet she was.

"The Bible says that each person is a sinner and everyone is wicked in the sight of God. God cannot allow sin into Heaven, so we must get rid of our sin somehow. If we don't, then we have no hope of Heaven." Luke found a side road, turned on it, and then pulled off to the side so they could talk without distraction.

"But how? I don't know how to get rid of my sin." The desperate look on her face was almost Luke's undoing.

He shook his head. "We can't get rid of our own sins, it's impossible." Then his eyes lit up. "But that's the beautiful thing about it, though. Jesus is the only one who can take our sins away. The Bible says that God is not willing that any should perish but that all should come to repentance. Jesus came down from Heaven and died on the cross for our sins."

"Someone died for *my* sins?" she asked as she closed her eyes and pictured the scene.

Luke turned in the seat to face her. "Not just *some*one. God's only begotten Son. He loved us enough to sacrifice His own life so that we could be saved. The Bible says that the blood of Jesus Christ cleanseth us from all sin."

"What a beautiful and terrible thing! I don't know what to say." Tears welled up in her eyes.

He took both of her hands in his. "Do you want to be free of your sins?"

"Yes, but at what cost? I'm not worthy to have someone die for me." She stared down at their hands, a tear slipped down her cheek.

"But Jesus already has. And the best part about it is He's not dead anymore. Three days after they buried Him, He arose from the dead. He's in Heaven sitting at the right hand of the Father."

Brianna's head spun. This was all so much to take in, to try to remember. "I want to go to Heaven too," she decided.

"*Gut*. Because I couldn't imagine it without you there by my side." He gave her a loving smile. "Just ask Jesus to save you and believe in what He did for you. God's Word says, 'For whosoever shall call upon the name of the Lord shall be saved.' His promises are always kept. He cannot lie."

She nodded. "Okay, I will." Brianna bowed her head and spoke aloud, "God, hello. This is Elisabeth. Luke told me about what you did for me and how Jesus died on the cross for my sins. I want to go to Heaven. Please take my sins away and save me. *Denki*. Amen."

As Luke looked into her tear-streaked face, his eyes clouded with tears as well. He pulled her into a hug and held her for several minutes. "I love you so much. I'm really happy that you've found the Lord."

Brianna melted at his words. "I want to marry you this fall," she said in a near whisper.

Luke immediately sat up and held her at arm's length. "You're sure?" At her nod, he drew her into his arms again and kissed her on the mouth. He knew it was wrong to compare earthly things to heavenly. But as far as he knew, this was as close to heaven on earth that he'd ever been. She said yes! Not only yes to him, but yes to God as well.

ELEVEN

*M*attie and Elisabeth both looked into the visor mirrors of Mattie's car before exiting. After making sure their makeup was just so and their hair was brushed properly, they walked into the bridal shop. Today would be the final fitting for their dresses: Mattie's bridal gown and Elisabeth's maid of honor dress. Mattie could scarcely believe she would be donning a thousand dollar wedding gown. And it had been one of the least expensive in the store. If she'd been married in her Mennonite community, her dress would have been self-sewn and wouldn't have cost more than a mere fifty dollars.

Mattie couldn't express how thankful she was to have Elisabeth by her side. She couldn't have asked for a better friend. Now they would both be marrying fancy *Englischers*, as they would have called them back home. Now they themselves were fancy *Englischers*.

"Hello, ladies!" a congenial sales representative greeted them. "Mattie Riehl, correct?"

"Yes, this is our final fitting." Mattie turned to Elisabeth and smiled.

"Ah, yes. I will grab your gowns from the back and meet you at the dressing rooms." With that, the woman made haste to the back of the store where the purchased dresses were kept. Mattie and Elisabeth made their way to the large dressing rooms.

"All right, ladies. I bet you're excited about the big day!" By the sound of it, one would think the salesclerk was the one getting married. She placed the dresses on the hooks of the private rooms. "Go ahead and try those on and I will be back in a few minutes to be sure they fit properly. Your petticoat is already in the room."

Mattie smiled exuberantly at Elisabeth and they both entered the fitting rooms to try their dresses on. "I'll probably need your help with the zipper."

"Okay, it shouldn't take me long to put my dress on and then I'll come in to help you," Elisabeth said before departing into the fitting room.

A couple of minutes later, Elisabeth joined Mattie in her dressing room. "*Ach*, Elisabeth! You look so beautiful in that dress. I think Carson's gonna faint dead away when he sees you."

Elisabeth laughed. "I don't think so. Now if *Luke* were to see me in it, he'd definitely faint dead away!"

Mattie giggled. "I think you're right. Red is not exactly an 'approved' Amish color, nor is that style of dress. But I know

Carson will love it, especially when he gets to dance with you at the reception."

"I'm a little nervous about that. I keep envisioning Bishop Hostettler walking into the reception hall and scolding us for being worldly," Elisabeth said, pulling up Mattie's zipper while she held her hair up.

Mattie giggled again. "Now, I don't remember *Grossdawdi* being that bad, but maybe Minister Fisher, Uncle Jonathan, was."

"You know they say the reason Minister Fisher is so serious about preaching is because he had a pretty wild past. I guess that explains the twins' behavior," she said wryly.

"Well, apparently he's quite different at home from what I've heard from my folks. He must be, otherwise they wouldn't have all those *kinner!*" Mattie laughed.

"*Ach*, if they only knew we were speaking of such things."

"That's good, though. You can't be that serious all the time. Do you think any of his *kinner* will go *Englisch?*" Mattie asked, ignoring Elisabeth's previous comment.

Lis shrugged. "You never know."

Mattie looked into the long mirror, experimenting with her hair. "How do you think I should do my hair? Should I wear it up or down?"

"How does Richard like it?"

"Down. He thinks the curls are cute." Mattie smiled.

"And so they are. Wear it down. Do you have your veil so we can see how it looks?" Elisabeth looked around the dressing room and spotted the veil on one of the wall hooks. "Here it is."

Mattie took the veil and placed it on top of her shoulder-length curly brown hair. "How about if I put half of it up? How does that look?"

"Perfect!" Elisabeth declared.

"After we're done with Richard's and my wedding, we're going to have go shopping to find you a wedding dress," Mattie commented.

"Oh, I don't think so. I wouldn't be able to afford anything like that. I'll have to check out some thrift stores," Lis said practically.

"You'll do no such thing! You can borrow mine if you'd like," Mattie offered kindly.

"I really appreciate that, Mattie, but I'm taller than you and my hips are a little wider." Elisabeth hoped her denial didn't dampen Mattie's spirit.

"I'm sure they can alter it for you," Mattie insisted.

"I'll think about it."

As Mattie and Elisabeth left the bridal shop, Mattie still couldn't get over the fact that her wedding was only a week away. It was a shame no one from home would be present to see her take her vows. The bittersweet thought brought tears to her eyes.

Brianna glanced over at Jacob who sat on the driver's side of their spring buggy. Jacob had been in a sullen mood since the youth gathering last weekend. When Brianna pushed him for answers, Jacob had brushed her off and told her to mind her own business. She still didn't know how the ride home went with her brother and Rachel, but she got the feeling it didn't go well.

"*Denki* for taking me to Rachel's, Jacob. It would have been too awkward for me to walk with all these baking supplies," Brianna said.

Jacob grunted. "It'd be better if you just learned to drive yourself, or had taken the cart along."

Brianna knew she could have done that, but it wouldn't have given Jacob and Rachel the opportunity to see each other. She was hoping that they could work out whatever was going on between them because she didn't like Jacob somber all the time. She much preferred his fun, teasing self. "Maybe you can teach me how to drive soon."

"*Jah.*" He shrugged.

The short ride only took a few minutes. When they pulled up to Rachel's, her friend opened the door and descended the porch steps to help unload. Jacob sat in the buggy and ignored the girls' cheerful greetings.

Brianna spoke up, "Jacob, will you help me take these things into the house please?"

Jacob sighed. "I'd think the two of you could handle that." When had her brother ever been so rude?

"There are some heavy things that we girls shouldn't be carrying. Please?" Brianna pleaded. She hoped stroking his ego might move him.

He grunted, "All right." It had worked.

Brianna smiled to herself and took some supplies into the house quickly, purposely leaving Rachel and Jacob outside alone together. She set the items on the kitchen table, and then stood by the door to eavesdrop on their conversation. She was sure she heard arguing.

"I hope you had a good time riding home with Jake Yoder," Jacob said accusingly.

So that's why Jacob has been in a bad mood. Rachel rejected his offer for a ride, Brianna realized.

"Well, I'm sure it was better than if I'd ridden home with you!" Rachel retorted.

Ouch! That wasn't very nice, Brianna thought.

"You would never have gone with me. Your *mamm* would never approve of it!" he sneered.

Rachel's tone became sober. "What's *that* supposed to mean, Jacob Schrock?" she said with her hands on hips.

"Oh, give me a break, Rachel!" Jacob bellowed, and then mimicked a woman's voice, "I'm sorry, Jacob, but I can't go riding with you anymore because my *mamm* won't let me."

Brianna had to stifle a giggle.

"So, that's what this is about?" Rachel replied tersely, "You're upset because my *mamm* won't let me ride with you?"

"We both know you're hiding behind your *mamm's* skirts, Rachel. Every time I ask you to do *anything*, you always have a reason why you can't."

"So, you think I've been making up all those excuses just to put you off?" Rachel said indignantly.

"Yes, I do!" Jacob shouted.

Brianna was beginning to think maybe this wasn't such a good idea after all.

"For your information, I *wanted* to ride home with you last Saturday! I only went with Jake Yoder because he asked me first. And when my *mamm* said I couldn't ride horses with you anymore, I ran upstairs to my room and cried for hours," Rachel admitted loudly.

Jacob stood there speechless as if trying to comprehend what she'd just told him. A minute ticked by in silence.

Brianna couldn't believe what she saw next.

Rachel forcefully grabbed Jacob's shirt and pulled him toward her. She then proceeded to give him a kiss like Brianna had never witnessed before, at least not that she could remember, right in front of her father's house! Jacob wrapped his arms around Rachel and they seemed lost in each other's embrace until Brianna figured she'd better break up the party before Rachel's father came in from the field and pulled out his hunting rifle.

Brianna cleared her throat before descending the steps. "Rachel, we'd better start baking before your *mamm* returns."

Jacob and Rachel broke apart, but stood gazing into each other's eyes.

Jacob spoke up, licking his lips, "Uh...yeah. I'll...I'll just go then." But instead of moving, his feet stayed planted to the ground.

"*Denki* for...uh...helping, Jacob." Rachel bit her bottom lip, seemingly bashful about her boldness now.

"Anytime." He tipped his hat, and then finally moved and hopped into his buggy.

Brianna could hear him whistle as he traveled toward home. She had to smile to herself, *it worked*!

TWELVE

Caroline Mitchell walked slowly down the hallway of the home she'd lived in since the birth of her first daughter nearly twenty-five years ago. She came to a bedroom door, reached out for the doorknob, and then stopped. Excruciating pain tore through her heart once again. It had been months since her daughter Brianna's passing, yet still she didn't have the strength to sort through her belongings. To do so would be dreadful for certain, it would also be final. It would force her to come to terms with the devastating plane crash that snatched her daughter away so suddenly. No, she wouldn't do it today. She wouldn't disturb the quiet sanctuary that had sat vacant for four months now.

As Elisabeth walked down the aisle, she caught Carson's eye. He was so attractive, standing next to Richard, in his black tuxedo. The red cummerbund and bowtie matched Elisabeth's dress precisely. Not many months hence she would be walking down the aisle in this same fashion. But next time *she* would be wearing the white dress, looking into the eyes of the man she'd be spending the rest of her life with, and longing for the honeymoon vacation that would follow.

She took her spot at the front of the altar as they'd rehearsed the day before, then watched in awe as the guests rose from their seats. The church pianist played the Bridal March and her best friend floated down the aisle with tears streaming down her cheeks. The wedding coordinator had informed them that the bride would normally be escorted by her father. Since that was not possible, Richard's father had stepped into the role, for which Mattie was grateful.

The ceremony was shorter than expected, especially since she was used to the three-hour-long Amish wedding ceremony. She'd caught Carson gazing at her several times while Mattie and Richard said their vows. She wondered if he was looking forward to their wedding day as much as she was.

Although Elisabeth wasn't accustomed to dancing, she acceded at Carson's prompting. She discovered that she enjoyed being held in his arms as they slowly swayed to the romantic music. But, as she'd been warned by the elders in her former Amish church, being in such close proximity to Carson, with his warm breath on her neck and their bodies nearly touching, had stirred feelings of desire that were better left alone until after they were wed. And even though Carson had wanted to dance to more songs, she had to decline for reasons she was uncomfortable discussing. Surely the Lord would not approve of such intimate desires.

"Do you know what kind of bridal gown you would like to wear?" Carson asked as he set his salad fork back onto his plate.

"I'm not sure. Mattie offered to let me borrow hers. I was thinking of doing that," Elisabeth said.

"You mean you wouldn't rather have your own dress? Not that Mattie's isn't nice, I just pictured you in something more elegant." Carson forked a bite of rice pilaf and chewed.

"They're just so expensive. I can't see myself paying that much money for a dress I'll only wear one time. I suppose I could look at the thrift stores." She shrugged.

"Oh no, you don't. No way. No bride of mine will be wearing a second-hand gown. I'm sorry Elisabeth, but no. I don't care how much your dress costs. I want you to go and pick something out that *you* like. I insist. I'm paying for it and I will hear no objections," he declared. "I love you and I want only the best for my bride."

Elisabeth's mouth hung open and she sat speechless. What could she say? He had spoken and there was no arguing. A sudden excitement sprung up in her soul as she thought about picking out her very own wedding dress – where price was a non-issue. Not that she'd ever pick something ridiculously expensive anyway. She was overwhelmed with gratitude and love for this special man who sat by her side. Tears welled up in her eyes as she spoke, "Thank you, Carson."

Brianna joined the baptism class with the other candidates during the church meeting on Sunday morning. Fortunately, Bishop Hostettler had allowed her to make up the classes she'd missed. As she learned the tenets of the faith, she became even more excited about her Christian walk. Since accepting Christ, Luke and she had regular Bible studies and discussions. It seemed that every day she learned more about God and His wondrous love.

Just two weeks hence, she and the others would be baptized in Millers' pond. Luke explained to her that before Bishop Hostettler's district broke off from Bishop Mast's district, baptism was performed according to the Old Order church tradition with the pouring of water into cupped hands and released over the believer's head. However, after the split the elders began searching the Scriptures diligently and realized that Biblical baptism indicated total immersion. Brianna was impressed by Bishop Hostettler's boldness at snuffing tradition to follow God's Word, surely it took gumption to break off and form a New Order.

Excitement and joy filled Brianna's heart at all that would take place in such a short time. She would soon be identifying with the Lord in believer's baptism and proclaiming to all that she is a follower of Christ. Soon she would begin sewing her wedding dress, and then be wed to the most wonderful man on earth. Her future couldn't be any brighter.

"I can't tell you how proud I am of you, Beth. Proud in a good way, I mean. You've grown and changed so much, I hardly recognize you from the old Elisabeth I used to know." Luke smiled, rowing the dory further out into Millers' pond.

"*Denki*, I think." Brianna smiled unsurely, leaning over and dipping her hand into the cool water.

Luke chuckled. "Don't worry. It's a *gut* thing for sure and for certain. You used to be so different – always kicking against the pricks, so to speak. I have to admit that you're much easier and more fun to love now. I don't know what happened to you when you were out in the world, but when you came back you were changed."

"Maybe it was a *gut* thing that I didn't remember who I was, *jah*? I guess God had a better plan for me than where I was headed, so he brought me back home," Brianna said thoughtfully.

"And I will be grateful to Him every day for that precious gift. He gave us a chance to start over, to start better. I am looking forward to spending my life with you, to showing you every day how much I love you, and to building a family with you. I can't wait to hold our first *kinner* in my arms." Luke's eyes sparkled with joy as they came to a stop at the small island in the middle of the pond. He hopped out of the boat and held out his hand to Brianna to help her out.

Panic suddenly seized Brianna. *Children? Of course, all Amish families had children – usually a lot of them.* Why had she never thought of this when Luke mentioned it before? The doctor's words played in her mind, "I am sorry, Miss Doe. But due to the extensive damage from the accident, you will most likely never be able to have children." At the time, the words hadn't meant much to her. They didn't hold any implications. But now? If she couldn't give Luke children then she would never be a proper wife. She could never be the wife that he wanted. She couldn't do this to him.

"Luke, I...I'm not feeling well now. Will you take me home?" Her hands shook and she hid them behind her back so he wouldn't see.

"But you seemed fine a minute ago. I don't understand. Did I say something?" He came and stood in front of her and raised her chin so that she had to look him in the eye.

She moved away and stood by the shore. "I just don't feel well now. I need to go home," her voice quavered and she couldn't help the lone tear that slipped down her cheek and dropped into the shallow water near her feet.

Concern shown in Luke's eyes and he moved toward her. "Something is wrong. Talk to me, Beth." He gently placed a hand on her shoulder.

She shook her head in defiance. How could she talk to him about this? He just said that he wanted children – probably lots of them. It wouldn't be fair to hold him back from his dreams, to deny him the opportunity to see his own offspring. She just didn't have the heart to do it. It grieved her heart at what she knew she must do. It would surely hurt them both now, but in the long run it would be best.

"We can't be together anymore, Luke." She hung her head and sobbed into her palms.

A knife cut through Luke's heart and he dropped his hand. "What do you mean?"

"We can't marry." She gathered her resolve and determined to remain strong, brushing away the tears.

"Why? You're not making any sense, Beth," Luke's voice raised an octave.

"I…I don't love you," she lied. Oh, it hurt so much to say the words. She hurried back into the boat. "Please just take me back."

"Beth, please."

The pain in Luke's voice was evident and she knew that he, too, was shedding tears. She couldn't give in no matter how much it hurt. Luke was a good man and deserved someone who could give him everything he wanted – and it wasn't her.

Luke quietly rowed the dory back to the shore. As soon as they landed, Brianna took off in a sprint toward home.

"Elisabeth, I don't know what I did or said, but please give me the chance to make it right," Luke called out after her, desperation in his voice.

Shutting out Luke's words, Brianna ran all the way home and cried until her tears ran dry. She didn't know what she would do now. Her future had all been planned out and now it crumbled in front of her. The thought of remaining single and alone was not appealing, but perhaps it was her only option as a barren Amish woman.

She closed the door to her bedroom and lay on her bed, exhausted by the day's events. Turning over on her side, she spotted her Bible on the night stand. With trembling hands she picked up the antiquated black book and opened it. Expecting to receive a rebuke, her heart lifted when she read the words on the page, "I will never leave thee, nor forsake thee."

"Thank you, God. Thank you for showing me that you'll always be there for me. I need you now more than ever. Please comfort my heart. And please be with Luke and take his pain away." As she finished the prayer, she drifted off into a fitful sleep.

THIRTEEN

"Elisabeth, you need to talk to Luke." Jacob stomped his foot, after placing his hat on the rack near the back mudroom. "What you're doing isn't fair."

Fair? What did he know about fairness? Was it fair that she'd never be able to have children? Was it fair that she had to leave Luke? Was it fair that she would probably have to stand by and watch the man she loves marry another? No, it wasn't fair. Not one bit. Jacob didn't understand. He had Rachel. Rachel was perfectly healthy, not flawed like she was.

"I don't want to talk to him. I have nothing to say," Brianna said frowning, swinging around to face him as she stood at the kitchen counter.

"Then talk to me, Lis," Jacob urged. "What's buggin' you? You're not the same, so I know something must've happened."

"It won't matter. I can talk until the moon turns purple and it won't solve anything." She turned her attention back to the dishes and sighed. "Please, just leave me alone."

"Fine. If you want to be left alone, then I'll leave you alone. But just remember that loneliness is a choice." He shook his head. "I can't believe you're turning Luke away. Can't you see that he cares for you? If you'd rather live a life of loneliness than with someone who loves you, I think you're *ferhoodled*." At that, Jacob stuffed his hat back on his head, turned, and walked out the door.

Brianna reached down into the basket and lifted out a pair of Michael's trousers. She enjoyed the time spent with *Mamm*, helping pin the wet laundry to the clothes line. The change of seasons was evident as a cool breeze blew through her hair, causing her *kapp* strings to fly. All around her, leaves were changing their hues. The green leaves of summer had turned, reminding her of Joseph's coat of many colors, sporting purple, red, orange, and gold. She breathed in the crisp autumn air, hoping the loveliness of nature would somehow cleanse her soul and overshadow her sorrow.

Mamm and *Dat* hadn't mentioned anything to her about the situation with Luke. Although he had come by several times, they respected her wishes and sent him away. She hoped that he would get over her soon, because he deserved somebody special. She suspected part of the reason her folks hadn't pressed her is because usually one of the other *kinner* was always around.

"I remember a time when your father and I were courting," her mother began, shaking the water residue from an apron before pinning it to the line, "we broke up for a time too."

Brianna watched as her mother was transported back into a time before she was born. "What happened?"

"I was scared of marrying your father. I thought that I would never be good enough for him, so I lied and told him that I didn't love him anymore," *Mamm* confessed.

How similar her situation was, Brianna thought. "What did he do?"

"Same as Luke, pretty much. Came around and tried to get me to talk to him, but I refused." *Mamm* laughed, taking *Dat*'s shirt out of the basket. "Oh, how stubborn I was. Everyone else around me could see that I still loved him, plain as day."

"So, what happened?" Brianna asked curiously.

"Well, God finally got ahold of me. I discovered that I needed to be truthful with myself, and with your *dat*, and with God. Running away from my problems wasn't going to help, nor make them go away. I wasn't trusting God. If I had, I would have been honest in the first place. It wonders me how we sometimes let fear take over our lives." *Mamm* placed a loving hand on Brianna's shoulder and smiled.

"But, what if your problems can't be solved?" Doubt flooded her mind as she considered sharing with her mother. She desperately needed to talk to someone about her troubles.

"There is no problem too large that God can't handle," *Mamm* assured. "Besides, God showed me a wonderful verse from His Word. Romans chapter eight verse twenty-eight: And we know that all things work together for good to them that love God, to them who are the called according to his purpose."

Brianna soaked in the verse, contemplating each word. "You mean that God can take something bad and make something good out of it?"

Mamm smiled and draped an arm around Brianna. "That's exactly what I mean."

"The doctor said I will probably never be able to have children." Tears clouded Brianna's eyes as she divulged her secret.

"So, that's what all this has been about," *Mamm* sympathized. "Have you told Luke?"

"No!" Brianna cried. "He wants *kinner.*"

"Don't you think you should let Luke decide whether he still wants to marry you or not?" *Mamm* raised an eyebrow. "You can't just call off your wedding and not give him a good reason. He has a right to make his own choices. Choices that are based on truth."

"But he'll be happier with someone else. Somebody who can give him children," Brianna asserted, brushing away another tear.

"No, I won't," a male voice echoed from behind her.

"Luke." Brianna startled. "How long have you been listening?"

"Long enough," he stated, walking purposefully toward the clothes line from the barn.

Mamm smiled at Brianna, picked up her empty basket, and disappeared into the house.

Luke came near, ducking under the clothes line. He took Brianna's hands in his. "You are enough for me, Beth. I love *you*. I don't want anybody else. I've never wanted anybody else." He stared into her troubled blue eyes, patiently waiting.

Brianna fell into his arms and wept, releasing her burden. Both tears of sorrow and tears of joy fell from her eyes. How could she be so happy and so sad all at the same time? "But what if we never have children?" She stepped back and searched his eyes.

"Then it will be as the Lord wills," he stated, gently stroking her damp cheek. "But doctors are not always right. And we can always adopt if we choose to."

Brianna looked up at Luke in disbelief. She knew she didn't deserve him. He was so good, so kind. "Have I ever told you how much I love you?" Her eyes shined with tears.

"Not today," he said, then bent down and lovingly pressed his lips to hers. "And one more thing, I spoke with Bishop Hostettler and our wedding date is scheduled for the first week in November."

"But that's just a few weeks away!" She gasped.

"I know. Isn't it wonderful?" He smiled broadly showing most of his beautiful pearly whites.

"*You* are wonderful!" Brianna giggled as Luke lifted her into the air and spun her around.

FOURTEEN

Elisabeth smiled with contentment as she watched the other diners. Most of them were obviously well-off, as evidenced by their attire. Women with fancy hairdos, strings of jewels, and the latest fashions accompanied men with well-tailored three-piece suits and shiny black shoes. It almost seemed as if they dressed just to impress the people around them. Unmistakably proud and fancy, indeed.

It sure was a far cry from where she'd come from. Pride, or *hochmut* as they called it, was definitely not an admirable quality in Paradise. Instead, the People valued humility, as the Lord exemplified while He was on earth. Plain dress was expected of all in her home community so as not to give one person more clout than another. A Bible verse that Elisabeth had heard her whole life popped into her mind, *Let nothing be done through strife or vainglory; but in lowliness of mind let each esteem other better than themselves.* She figured the verse probably went both ways. It was surely possible to have 'Plain pride' as well.

Elisabeth looked down at her own clothing in comparison. Although it wasn't anywhere near as flashy as some of the ladies' in the restaurant, it definitely wouldn't be considered Plain. She felt it was a good compromise between the two worlds – modest yet stylish. And it complemented Carson's collared button-down and pressed slacks.

There was one thing that she felt was a little out of place though. She looked at her left hand, espying her fancy diamond ring. It was unquestionably more exquisite than what she would have chosen for herself. She cringed at the thought of what Carson may have paid for it. Mattie had guessed upwards of ten thousand dollars, being that it was one and a half carats. Elisabeth didn't doubt that, since Carson seemed so blasé when it came to money. It was obvious that he owned his money as opposed to letting his money own him. Her lack of money didn't seem to bother Carson one bit, and for that she was thankful.

"This is a very nice restaurant," Elisabeth commented as she perused the high-priced menu.

Carson lifted a brow. "You don't mind, do you? I know we usually don't eat at places this extravagant, but I wanted to treat my fiancée to something special."

"Oh no, it's fine." She smiled. "So, are the prices any indication of the quality of food?"

Carson laughed. "We shall see. I like it because they have some pretty awesome vegan entrees."

"I figured they must've had some. So, what do you suggest?" She turned to the vegan section of the menu.

"You're going to be brave enough to try something vegan?" Elisabeth laughed at Carson's surprised tone.

"Maybe," she teased.

"Well, my favorite is the grilled barbequed seitan skewers with wild mushroom pate." He rolled his eyes with pleasure, reminding her of her brother's dog Barney when someone would scratch him on the belly.

Elisabeth's eyes widened. "Grilled Satan?"

Carson caught her confusion and laughed out loud. "No, not Satan like the devil, seitan as in the food. It's made from wheat gluten and is used as a type of meat substitute. You spell it s-e-i-t-a-n."

Elisabeth laughed as well.

"But you especially have to try the chocolate lava cake, it's absolutely delectable." Carson could already taste the gooey sweetness.

"Hmm…Satan and lava. Have you been reading Revelation twenty again?"

Carson couldn't help but laugh again. "Are you referring to the passage where the devil is thrown into the lake of fire? Almost sounds like it, huh?"

Conversation was interrupted when a couple about her parents' age approached their table. "Brianna!" the woman shrieked, and everyone in the restaurant turned their gazes in the direction of their table.

Carson immediately spoke up, "No, Mrs. Mitchell. This is not your daughter. I thought Elisabeth was Brianna too, when I first saw her."

"Oh my!" The woman's eyes clouded with tears. "Are you sure? She looks identical to our Brianna. She could easily be her twin."

"Please, Mr. and Mrs. Mitchell, meet my fiancée Elisabeth." Carson stood from the table to greet Brianna's parents.

Elisabeth stood and politely held out her hand, noticing that the woman couldn't take her eyes off her face. "Nice to meet you."

"Forgive my wife and me, please. We are just a little overwhelmed," Mr. Mitchell said as he shook her hand.

"I understand," she said sympathetically. She could only imagine how painful it must be for Brianna's parents. "I'm sorry for your loss."

"Thank you, dear," Mrs. Mitchell replied, attempting to regain control over her emotions. "It was a pleasure meeting you."

"Congratulations on your engagement, Carson." The man nodded politely, and then turned to his wife. "Caroline, shall we return to our table?" The woman agreed and Brianna's parents disappeared into another section of the restaurant. But Elisabeth noticed that Caroline watched her every step of the way.

After seeing Jacob in the barn for few minutes, he informed Rachel that his parents had gone into Lancaster. Jacob urged her to stay and spend some time with him up in the haymow. Although the idea was awfully tempting, she decided it wasn't a very good idea for them to be alone together. Not only did she not trust him, but she didn't trust herself as well. She'd decided years ago that when she married, she wanted to be pure for her husband. And as hard as it was to stay away from Jacob, she knew that's what she had to do to remain pure. She would have been fooling herself to think otherwise. After the day Jacob had shown up at her house with Brianna, the two had gone on several buggy rides and were officially courting now.

Rachel knocked on the back door of the Schrocks' home, not hearing a response. Since she knew Brianna was in the house, she let herself inside. The smell of fresh baked bread permeated the room, tantalizing her nostrils. Rachel smiled, thinking of the baking lessons she'd been giving Brianna. Her first attempts at baking bread had been amusing. One batch of dough rose so high in the loaf pan, it blossomed over the top and spilled onto the counter. Another batch had come out of the oven hard as a brick. But eventually Brianna had gotten it right and at the end of the day, she was confident that she'd be able to provide fresh bread for her family.

Rachel plodded up the stairs to Brianna's bedroom and knocked on the door. Brianna smiled and gave her friend a hug, welcoming her to her private sanctuary. "Are you excited about joining the church this Sunday?" Rachel asked her good friend.

"*Ach*, yes! I've just been reading over the verses on baptism and the importance of meeting together with believers." Brianna closed her Bible and set it back on the small nightstand.

"I remember how excited I was when I joined the church last year." Rachel's eyes lit up. "I think Luke and Jacob were baptized at the same time."

Brianna frowned. "I'm sorry I missed it. I should have been here. I would like to have seen that."

"Don't worry about what's in the past because there's nothing you can do to change it. None of us has been perfect." Rachel absentmindedly ran her hand over the pattern on the quilt where she sat on the bed. "We just have to live each new day as if it's a precious gift. When I wake up in the morning I like to think that this day will be better than any day I've ever lived." Rachel laughed, and then continued, "And it is because I haven't made any mistakes yet."

"Luke said that God doesn't even remember our sins. I think that's pretty amazing." Brianna sighed. "I wish I could forget my foolish mistakes."

"And their sins and iniquities will I remember no more," Rachel quoted the verses, "As far as the east is from the west, so far hath he removed our transgressions from us."

"I love those verses. Please tell me where they're from so I can memorize them," Brianna requested, reaching for her Bible and a pen.

Rachel put a finger over her lips trying to recall the references. "I'm not exactly sure. I think the first one is found in Hebrews somewhere and the second is Psalm one hundred three."

Brianna quickly jotted down some notes.

Rachel looked over at a heap of blue material stacked on Brianna's dresser and her eyes lit up. "Is that for your wedding dress?"

Brianna frowned. "*Jah.*"

"What's wrong?" Rachel laughed at her friend's disenchanted expression.

"Everything!" Brianna whimpered, "I can't remember how to sew and I'm supposed to have this done already."

"Didn't your *mamm* show you how?" Her face seemed flabbergasted.

"*Jah*, she helped me sew some pants for the boys so I should be able to make some for Luke. But...I've never made a whole dress by myself," she cried. "I just don't want to mess it up. And there's the cape and apron to sew also."

"And your *kapp*," Rachel reminded, and then made up her mind. "All right, get out all your material and let's go sew your dress."

"But Rachel —" Brianna began to protest.

"Don't even try to argue with me, Lis. It doesn't work for your brother and it won't work for you either," Rachel insisted.

Brianna held in a chuckle. She had already seen Jacob attempting to argue with Rachel and it was obvious who had the upper hand. Her brother and Rachel were absolutely perfect for each other.

The rest of the morning and afternoon Rachel and Brianna worked on her wedding dress. Rachel showed Brianna how to measure and cut out the material, which pieces to sew first, and how to make sure it all fit together properly. When late afternoon approached, Brianna's new dress and apron were ready to try on.

"*Ach*, Elisabeth. You look so *schee*," Rachel exclaimed.

Brianna laughed remembering her mistaken word prior to arriving back home. "Just as long as I don't look like *schnee*."

Rachel giggled. "I remember that. You've been doing much better with your *Dietsch*."

"Well, I better change out of this before somebody comes home and sees me in it." Brianna smiled dreamily, picturing her wedding day.

"Yes. And I better go spend some time with your brother before he comes in here and bothers us again." Rachel laughed. "I think he's jealous of all the time I spent with you today."

"Just remind him that you were my friend first." Brianna giggled as well, and then gave Rachel a warm hug. "*Denki* for everything, Rachel. You are a very *gut* friend."

"Hey, save some of that for me!" Jacob hollered from the door.

Rachel winked at Brianna. "See what I mean?"

As Jacob and Rachel closed the door behind them, Brianna went back upstairs to her bedroom to daydream about Luke's and her wedding day.

FIFTEEN

Frank Mitchell glanced up from his newspaper and watched his wife as she stared into space. The loss of their daughter had deeply impacted both of them, but it seemed his wife had a more difficult time letting Brianna go. Ever since they'd seen Carson's fiancée at the restaurant, Caroline had been different. Frank knew she was probably dreaming that Elisabeth was indeed Brianna. He himself couldn't help but wonder about their astonishing resemblance. But something had to be done.

"Caroline?" Frank gently set the newspaper down on the end table beside the couch. "I think it's time we sort through Brianna's things."

Caroline covered her face with her hands and shook her head. "I don't know if I can do it."

"We must move on. Our daughter is not coming back," Frank's voice shook as he painfully voiced the reality.

"I...I can't. Not yet." She leaned on her husband's strong arm.

"Carson has been able to move forward. Don't you think we should too?" He put his hand on his wife's back and lovingly began soothing her tense muscles. "Why don't we call Ashley? She'd probably be willing to sort through her sister's things with you."

Caroline nodded her head. "She's already urged me to do it. I know she won't mind."

"I think her being here will help to lessen some of the pain for you as well. Would you like me to call?" Frank suggested.

Releasing a pent-up sigh, his wife relinquished a slight nod.

Frank rose to telephone their daughter and returned a few minutes later. "Ashley will be coming over in a few weeks. I'd forgotten they were going to be out of town for a while."

"That's right. She and Hayden were going to take the children to that theme park." Caroline remembered. "Perhaps we can get it done before Thanksgiving."

"I think that would be a good idea." Frank picked up the paper again and nodded.

"Mattie Riehl!" the sales representative greeted as Mattie and Elisabeth entered the bridal boutique.

Mattie beamed. "I'm Mrs. Mattie Greene now." She held up her left hand, showing off her shiny new wedding ring.

"That's right. Congratulations! Did you have an enjoyable time on your honeymoon?" the bubbly woman enquired.

"Oh, yes! We went on a seven-day cruise to the Caribbean Islands. It was so beautiful, I felt as if I was experiencing a piece of Heaven! Everything about it was magnificent, although I feel like I gained about ten pounds from the exuberant amount of delicious food available." She laughed.

"I've heard that cruises are a lot of fun, but I've yet to embark." The woman smiled. "Now, what did you ladies come into the store for today?"

Mattie gestured to Elisabeth, trying to contain her excitement. "My friend is getting married!"

"That's wonderful. When's the big day?"

"We're planning the wedding for spring. It will give us some time to prepare," Elisabeth said. "After helping Mattie with hers, I've seen how much time goes into it and how much preparation it takes."

"That's right, you can never start planning too early. Now, what style of dress are you looking for?" The sales lady eyed Elisabeth, seemingly assessing her size.

"I want something modest. Not too form fitting and without too much embellishment." Elisabeth decided.

"I think I have just the thing for you." The woman led the way to a rack of endless white gowns. "You'll see that there are several here that meet your description, but I think you'd look fabulous in this one." She pulled the most expensive gown off the rack.

Elisabeth's eyes bulged when she saw the price. "That one is little too fancy for my taste." She didn't particularly care for the dress any way.

Another customer entered the store and the sales woman turned to leave. "I'll just leave you two to look and you can let me know if you need anything."

Mattie turned to Elisabeth. "Have you thought about bridesmaids' dresses?"

"Yes, I have." Elisabeth happily dragged Mattie over to a far wall. "What do you think of this?" She held out a lime green calf-length dress.

"Is that what you want?" Mattie raised her eyebrows.

Elisabeth nodded enthusiastically.

"I think it's pretty," she said in a cautioned tone.

"But?"

"It's just so non-Amish," Mattie admitted.

"That's exactly why I like it. We would never be able to wear a dress this color back home," Elisabeth noted. "I want to embrace and enjoy my freedom. Not that I would ever dress like some of the *Englischers* we've seen."

"I know what you mean. It's nice to be able to wear something that *you* like and that you've picked out yourself, as opposed to having all of the choices made for you," Mattie expressed.

"Right. So, do you like it?" Elisabeth awaited Mattie's reply with anticipation.

"I absolutely love it!" Mattie exclaimed.

A nervous excitement permeated the room as Deacon Yoder announced the candidates for baptism. Brianna, along with three other young women and three young men, sat on the front chairs in the home of Joshua and Annie Hostettler. Brianna discreetly looked around and found Luke sitting in the second row next to her brothers. He caught her eye and sent her a quick wink. She'd never been to a baptism before so she wasn't exactly sure what to expect, although Rachel had explained the process to her.

After the three-hour service, the candidates would rise and go into a designated room to change into special baptismal garments. Then the candidates, along with Bishop Judah Hostettler, Minister Fisher, and Minister Esh, would lead the way to Millers' pond. There each candidate would again confirm his or her profession of faith in Jesus Christ, and one by one be baptized fully in the water.

Rachel had also informed Brianna of the Old Order Amish baptismal traditions wherein water would simply be poured over the heads of the candidates, as Luke had told her previously. Rachel noted that the Old Order frowned upon their 'modern' practices of baptism, although it was first practiced when John the Baptist walked the earth.

Brianna's excitement rose when Minister Esh called her into the water. She slowly walked out to where the leaders stood, the cool water rose to her waist, momentarily stealing her breath away. Bishop Hostettler explained that baptism was not the means by which one is saved, but simply an outward sign of salvation. Just as an Amishman's beard is an indication of his marriage and commitment to his wife, so baptism symbolizes our covenant with Christ.

Emerging from the water, Brianna couldn't hide the smile on her face. She had just participated in one of the ordinances that Christ himself practiced and ordained when He was here on earth. Now she felt a common kinship with her community as well. She would now be a voting member of the church, and of course, now she could marry the man of her dreams.

SIXTEEN

Brianna had just turned in for the night when she heard a small plunk outside her window. She smiled. *Luke.* Confirming her suspicion, she looked down to see him standing with something under his arm. Brianna waved at him and indicated she would be down shortly to let him in.

After dressing in short order, Brianna quietly flew down the stairs to meet her love. She stepped outside onto the porch and was immediately enveloped in Luke's embrace. His sweet kiss made her weak in the knees.

"Thanks for not screaming at me this time." He chuckled.

Brianna's cheeks flushed at the remembrance.

"I brought something for you." Luke grinned, gesturing toward the package on the swing.

"Would you like to go inside?" Brianna offered, remembering her mother's instructions on what to do when a beau summoned her from outside the bedroom window. "I can fix us some hot cocoa."

"In a little bit. Let's stay out under the stars and admire God's handiwork for a while, *jah*?" Luke suggested.

"Should we sit on the porch or go for a walk?"

Luke grasped her hand and led her down the steps. "Let's walk. You can open your package later when we go inside."

Brianna looked up into the clear night, awed by the abundance of radiant light above them. Luke pointed out several constellations, telling her stories about each one.

"Did you know that some people think the message of the Bible is written in the stars?" Luke asked.

"*Ach*, really? How?" This was the first time Brianna had heard such a thing.

"They say that the constellation Virgo got its name because of the Virgin Mary. Leo, which means lion, represents Christ, called the Lion of Judah." He pointed out.

"That's amazing. Is it true?" Brianna asked wide-eyed.

Luke shrugged his shoulders. "I'm not sure. I borrowed a book on the subject from the library one time. It made a lot of sense. The theory states that before the Scriptures were written, God put the Gospel in the stars. They think God revealed his plan to Adam, who passed it on to subsequent generations."

"Wow, I think it's fascinating." Brianna marveled, and then slightly shivered.

Luke immediately took off his jacket and wrapped it around her. "You're cold. Let's go have some hot cocoa now, *jah*?"

She smiled, not just because of the gift that awaited her, but because Luke's warm garment around her permeated her senses. She wished she could keep his scent with her forever. "That sounds *gut*. I can't wait to open my gift." Brianna and Luke walked back up to the house and went inside.

While Brianna prepared the cocoa in the kitchen, Luke stoked the fire in the living room. Brianna entered the living room with mugs in hand and cautioned. "We may have to wait a little while, it's very hot."

"*Gut*." Luke smiled and handed her the gift. "You can open this now."

Rachel had previously informed Brianna that oftentimes a beau would bring a gift to his *aldi* prior to their wedding day as a type of engagement present. She had said that the gift was usually something for the home, and that traditionally most young men gave a clock.

Brianna smiled, taking the gift from Luke's hands. She quickly removed the plain brown packaging and imagined Luke lovingly wrapping the gift for her. "Did you wrap this yourself?" she asked curiously.

"*Jah*, I did," he answered, seeming a bit shy.

Brianna wondered if he was self-conscious about his wrapping abilities. "You did a *gut* job," she reassured him, and then opened up the box, removing a beautiful clock. The masterpiece had a porcelain base with a large glass dome protecting the timepiece inside. Small butterflies and flowers graced the porcelain bottom and a silver pendulum rotated in sequence to the ticking of the second hand. Brianna had never seen anything more lovely.

"Luke, it's wonderful! I've never seen a clock so pretty." Her smile lit up the darkened room.

"I hoped you'd like it." He grinned. "It's called an anniversary clock, so I thought that every time we look at it we would think of our wedding day."

"I'll think of this day, too. *Denki*, Luke. I love you." She leaned over and gave him a well-deserved kiss.

"And to think we'll be married this time next week. Are you as excited as I am?" Luke took a sip of his hot cocoa.

"Maybe more." She smiled. "A little nervous too."

Luke said nothing and nodded. He wondered if perhaps she wasn't just nervous about the wedding itself, but also about the wedding night. He admitted to himself that he was a little nervous about it too, but figured that matter would take care of itself. After all, it was the way God designed things to be.

"Would you like some cookies?" Brianna offered.

"*Nee, denki*," Luke answered. "I have some news that I think you'd like to hear."

Brianna's eyes perked up.

"Jacob came and talked to me today. He asked Rachel to marry him and they're getting married two days after us." His eyes danced, waiting for her reaction.

"*Ach*, no!" she said in disbelief. "Rachel didn't say anything, and I didn't hear Deacon Yoder publish it at meeting."

"He just asked her, so we're the only ones that know. Jacob said they'll probably be published this Sunday," Luke explained.

"I didn't know they'd want to get married this soon, but I can't say that I blame them. Just think, my brother getting married to my best friend." Brianna smiled.

"Well, it's not much different than your brother's best friend marrying his sister," Luke commented, reaching for her hand.

"I'm so happy for them. And for us." She squeezed his hand. A sudden frown crossed her face. "But, we won't get to attend their wedding. We'll be visiting our relatives."

"I've got that all planned out. We won't leave for my cousin's district until after Jacob and Rachel's wedding. I knew you wouldn't want to miss it and neither do I. Besides, it will give us a couple of days to move your things to our place and get settled a bit before we set off," Luke stated.

He's going to make such a fine husband. Brianna smiled as she finished her cocoa. *Less than a week! I can hardly wait.*

Rachel, Brianna, and her mother sat around the kitchen table going over a check-off list of last minute wedding preparations. "Luke's asked the Weavers, the Yoders, the Brennemans, the Spencers, and the Hostettlers to help with preparing and serving the meal. Do you think that will be enough?" Brianna looked her mother's way.

She counted on her fingers. "*Jah*, that ought to do. Do Luke's parents have the necessary fowl?" her mother asked.

"They have five ducks, ten hens, and eight turkeys. I think that will be enough with what we have. I just hope there will still be plenty for Jacob and Rachel's wedding." She glanced Rachel's way, checking the birds off of the list.

"*Ach*, that will be fine. *Mamm* has plenty to spare," Rachel assured, peeking out the window for a glimpse of her man.

"Rachel, will your sister and *Mamm* still be joining us for preparations the day before?" Brianna was becoming more tense as the day grew closer. It seemed there was so much to do.

Rachel nodded.

"Luke and Jacob will be painting tomorrow. The benches should arrive on Friday. Yours and Rachel's dresses are finished. We'll pick the celery on Saturday so it will be fresh. Abigail Miller, Susanna Fisher, and Maryanna Riehl have all volunteered to bake pies and cakes. I think we've pretty much got everything covered." *Mamm* Schrock smiled satisfactorily. She rubbed a loving hand down Brianna's back, a tear graced her cheek. "I'm so happy my Elisabeth is getting married. And to such a fine man as Luke Beiler."

Brianna and Rachel also teared up.

Then *Mamm* Schrock took Rachel's hand. "And my Jacob has also found a *gut maedel.*"

"I hope to make a *gut fraa* for your son." Rachel smiled.

"You will, *Dochder.*" She smiled reassuringly.

SEVENTEEN

Brianna had never been more nervous or excited in her life. Today she would marry Luke Beiler. Kind, handsome, loving Luke. It was no doubt a dream come true. As far as she knew, she was the most blessed woman in the world. She was certain that nothing in the whole world could dampen her spirits today. Nothing could make her happier than becoming Mrs. Elisabeth Beiler.

While she and Rachel dressed in her bedroom, Jacob and Luke donned their wedding attire down the hall in Jacob's room. Soon the two couples would join and meet downstairs for the three-hour long ceremony. Everything was prepared, and so far everything was absolutely perfect.

Brianna and Luke, along with Jacob and Rachel, walked down a center aisle to the front of the room where the ministers sat and took their seats. A song leader rose to his feet and began the first note of a song, to which the remainder of the congregation joined in. Bishop Hostettler rose from his seat indicating to Luke and Brianna it was time to receive their final private marriage instructions. They followed the bishop to an upstairs room as the remainder of the congregation continued to sing. After the couple had finished their instruction in the proper Biblical duties of a husband and wife, they rejoined their guests downstairs for the continuation of the ceremony.

A long sermon began noting several couples from the Bible beginning with Adam and Eve. Warnings were also given about making and breaking vows, indicating that the only way out of a marriage was death. The husband was encouraged to love his wife as Christ loved the church and the wife was admonished to submit to and reverence her husband. When the sermon was completed, the couple was beckoned to come forward and stand before the minister.

As Luke and Brianna stood before Bishop Hostettler, he joined their hands together. They made their vows promising to love and cherish one another, come what may. A closing song and prayer was offered. Brianna and Luke were now officially husband and wife, and both were thrilled with their new reality.

The new couple was soon whisked off by horse and buggy to the home of Andrew Lapp, who was their second nearest neighbor. The Schrocks' closest neighbors were the Brennemans, but due to Jacob and Rachel's upcoming wedding, it had been decided to have the meal at the Lapps' property. A wedding feast of roasted fowl, stuffing, creamed celery, potatoes, and various side dishes were served first to the newlyweds and then to their guests. Several seating sessions had been necessary due to limited space and the upwards of four hundred well-wishers in attendance. After a second, more simple meal in the evening, the young people gathered in the barn for singing and games. The festivities ran long into the night, leaving Brianna and Luke exhausted, but yet elated, by the end of the day. Their journey as one had begun with hearts full of joy.

"I'm glad we came here today. The weather's perfect for a nice fall picnic," Elisabeth mentioned as she and Carson unfolded the large quilt she'd brought along for them to sit on. It was the first picnic she'd been on with Carson, as it seemed he mostly preferred restaurants.

Elisabeth heard the squeak of a swing set nearby and pleasant Amish one-room schoolhouse memories came rushing back. Children's laughter filled the air as she removed a few sandwiches from a wicker picnic basket. Joy filled her heart as she realized she would soon begin her own family. She was certain Carson would make a fine father.

"Yes, it's unseasonably warm today. It seems like forever since I've been on a picnic." He plopped down on the blanket, and then sprawled out on his back. "This sunshine feels great," he said as he propped his head up on one elbow facing Elisabeth.

"So, when was the last time you went on a picnic?" She smiled, handing him an eggless tofu sandwich.

"Hmm…" He thought a moment, scratching his head. "I think I must've been about ten years old. How about you?"

Elisabeth wondered if she should mention Luke, and then decided honesty was the best policy. "A couple of years ago." She shrugged.

Carson's eyebrows rose. "Really? Would that have been with a man?"

"Luke. He was my beau. He's still Amish as far as I know," she said.

Carson sat up and inched toward Elisabeth, assessing her eyes. "I'm sorry I asked. Hopefully, you won't be thinking of him now." He bent down, closing his eyes, and gently brushed his lips to hers.

"How could I, with such a wonderful man by my side?" She smiled and kissed him again. She was just about to hand Carson a bag of carrot sticks when a soccer ball sailed into his leg.

A girl approximately eight years old shyly entered their personal space to retrieve the ball. Elisabeth smiled, thinking of her younger sisters.

Before Carson handed her the ball, he warned sternly, "Make sure this doesn't happen again. Be more careful next time."

Elisabeth's eyes widened in horror as the little girl's eyes filled with tears at the harsh rebuke. The girl ran away, soccer ball in hand, no doubt to complain to her guardian about the mean man.

"How could you say that? She didn't aim the ball at you on purpose," Elisabeth confronted him.

"Kids should be more respectful of others, especially adults," he stated, shaking his head in disgust.

"You...you don't like children?" Elisabeth stumbled over the words.

"They're fine sometimes, I guess." He shrugged insouciantly.

"Fine? Sometimes? I hope you don't have that view of your own children," she said, still unbelieving of this alien in front of her.

"My own children?" He appeared shocked. "I don't have any children."

"But surely you want some." Suddenly, the differences between the *Englisch* world and the Amish became obvious. Just as a large gaping hole in her mother's favorite quilt.

He shook his head. "Not really. But I guess if *you* want one..."

"One?" Her eyes bulged. Elisabeth thought of her seven brothers and sisters at home. She couldn't imagine just having one child. In fact, she'd always dreamed of having at least a dozen. Her heart plummeted. There was no way she could marry this man.

"What's wrong?" Carson placed a hand on her shoulder.

She shrugged it off. "Everything. I can't marry you, Carson." She quickly began putting all the food items back into the basket, hoping to leave. The sooner the better.

"Wait a minute. What do you mean? You don't want to marry me now because I don't want children?" He ran a hand through his hair, seemingly incensed.

"That's right. I won't be happy with just one child, Carson," she insisted.

He scratched his head, trying to figure a way to work this out. He gave in. "I guess two would be all right."

"You don't understand. I don't want one or two. Please just take me home now, Carson." She crossed her arms, indicating the discussion was over. Honestly, she was ready to go home and have a good cry. The man of her dreams was far from what she thought he was. Her perfect *Englisch* life was quickly becoming a nightmare.

Resigned, Carson said no more and they rode to her apartment in silence. Elisabeth gathered the picnic basket and quilt, and then slid the shiny ring off her finger. She handed it to Carson. He held his hand up in protest, not accepting the ring. "Let's talk about this, Elisabeth." His eyes pleaded.

As far as she was concerned, there was nothing to discuss. It was obvious marriage between the two of them would never work. When he still refused to take the ring, she set it down on the passenger seat. "Goodbye, Carson." She closed the door and then turned before he could see the tears fall from her eyes.

Caroline's hands shook as she opened the door to welcome Ashley into her home. She had been dreading this day. Not because her daughter was visiting, but because her other daughter would never visit again.

Ashley embraced her mother when she noticed her reticence. "We all miss her, Mom." She wiped a tear from her eye.

"I never should have let her go to visit Heidi. If I would have insisted she stay home, she'd still be here." Caroline sniffled.

"Mom, you can't blame yourself. It's not your fault. You had nothing to do with that plane going down, you didn't know," Ashley reassured and rubbed her mother's back. "Besides, blaming yourself won't bring her back to us."

Caroline looked up. "You're right. I'm glad I still have you. Thank you for coming today. I don't think I could do this alone."

"Let's get started. I think the sooner we get this over with, the better. Brianna wouldn't have wanted you to carry on like this. She would want you to move on with your life," Ashley maintained, as she led the way to her sister's former room.

Ashley swung the door open and a wash of memories assaulted her. Brianna's scent still permeated the room. She smiled as she noticed the Barbie hotel sitting on the floor in a corner. Oh, the hours she and Brianna would sit and play with their Barbie dolls. Barbie always arrived in her pink Corvette and was greeted by Ken, who descended his hotel room in the ultra-cool pulley elevator. Tears flooded her eyes. This was going to be more difficult than she'd realized.

"Do you have any boxes, Mom? We should probably empty her closet and drawers and give the items to the Salvation Army." Ashley surveyed the room.

"Yes, I will get them." Caroline returned a minute later with several cardboard boxes.

"Do you mind if I keep a few things?" Ashley thought about her daughters enjoying the vintage toys in the future.

"Of course not, you take whatever you'd like to have. I will probably just keep her photos," her mother stated. "Where should we start?"

"Let's tackle the closet first, and then we can empty her drawers."

Empty. That's how my heart has felt since Brianna has been gone. Caroline wiped away a tear as she opened the closet door. Brianna's tops, sweaters, and jackets lined the upper section of the walk-in closet, and skirts and pants filled the bottom dowels. They removed each item from its hanger and reverently placed them into the boxes. Caroline decided to keep one of Brianna's favorite sweatshirts and laid it on the bed. Many shoes and boots filled the shelves, but soon the closet became an empty shell.

Ashley glanced around the room to see what area to tackle next. Brianna's red suitcase in the corner caught her eye. "Mom, what luggage did Brianna take with her?"

"I believe she took her red suitcase and carry-on bag," Caroline said. "She didn't have any other."

"Isn't that her luggage?" Ashley pointed to the corner.

Caroline's eyes widened, and then her brow creased in confusion. "Yes, it is."

Both women hurried to the red bags and Ashley set the suitcase on the bed. She quickly unzipped the bag and found Brianna's clothes inside. "I don't understand. Did she forget all her clothes?" Ashley wore a puzzled look.

Caroline picked up the carry-on bag and unzipped it as well. She gasped. "Her purse! You don't think she'd leave without her purse, do you?"

Ashley picked up the brown leather satchel and quickly emptied its contents. "Mom, her wallet and passport are here! She couldn't have gotten on the airplane without these."

Caroline and Ashley stared at each other in disbelief wondering what to think. Caroline spoke, "Do you think she could have missed her flight?"

"After Nine-Eleven there's no way they would have let her board that plane. No passport, no I.D." Ashley thought for another moment. "Mom, did you ever see an official passenger list from Brianna's flight?"

Caroline shook her head. "No."

"And they never found her body?" Ashley dared to get her hopes up.

"No, but they said it's common not to recover bodies of victims lost in the ocean," Caroline contended.

"We need to call the airline or the FAA or someone to get a copy of the passenger list, because by the look of it Brianna never got on that plane," Ashley asserted.

EIGHTEEN

A light snow covered the ground on Thanksgiving Day, but not enough to utilize the cutter. Luke was looking forward to the winter months when he and his new wife would be snowed in, sharing special moments together, nestled by the fireplace. He remembered how, as a child, he loved to go for a ride in his father's cutter. A pain filled his heart at the stark reality that he and Elisabeth would most likely be childless. He'd always imagined being married to Elisabeth and having miniature likenesses of the two of them running around, bringing joy to their hearts. But at least he had Elisabeth, what more could he ask for?

As he prepared the buggy to ride over to the Schrocks' house, he'd thought of their marriage so far. They'd gotten along better than he expected. Elisabeth used to demand her way and challenge him, sometimes causing his anger to flare. But ever since she returned from New York, she had been different, like a whole new person. Luke liked the changes, though. He realized he was glad they had waited to marry because it'd given them both time to mature. He was certain that if they'd married earlier in life they would have never gotten along as well as they do.

Elisabeth definitely wasn't as deft in the kitchen as she used to be, but he didn't mind her mishaps. He understood that the accident had taken a lot from her and it would take time to learn all of the skills she had forgotten. It made him realize all the simple things he took for granted. Yes, he had a lot to be thankful for.

Luke tethered the horse to the hitching post and marched joyfully up the back porch steps. The delightful aroma of peanut butter oatmeal cookies permeated the air. He spotted his wife near the sink and strode up behind her, wrapping his arms around her trim waist. "Have I ever told you how thankful I am to have you as my wife, Beth?" He nuzzled his nose against her neck.

Brianna turned around in his arms and giggled. "Only every day. But I don't ever tire of hearing it."

He bent down to meet her lips. "Nor I of saying it."

After a few deliciously tantalizing moments in his wife's embrace, he figured they'd better go before they showed up late. Again. They ended up nearly missing the last supper with his parents because they'd gotten a little too carried away in the passion department. Of course, instances like that were to sometimes be expected with newlyweds but not too often. Thankfully, their families tended to be a little more understanding than most Amish households. There was a time and a place for everything, and while the place was right, the timing had definitely been off. He wouldn't have his wife show up embarrassed and rosy-cheeked at her folks' home on this special day.

Within short order, everything was loaded up, Elisabeth snuggled beside him in the buggy, and they were on their way to spend Thanksgiving dinner with her family. Since he and Jacob were good friends he always enjoyed time spent at the Schrock home. He was equally glad that Elisabeth would have her best friend Rachel present as well. The newlywed couple had moved into the small *dawdi haus* connected to the Schrocks' main dwelling. Luke was glad for the extra privacy having his own home provided.

The couple was greeted with smiles and hugs as they merrily entered Elisabeth's childhood home. Luke noticed that Jacob seemed happier than his usual self and knew that married life had been good to him too. Rachel, on the other hand, seemed a little pale and he wondered if perhaps she was under the weather.

The menfolk congregated out in the barn while the womenfolk put the finishing touches on the meal and set the table. Children played games around the stove in the living room as they waited for the food.

When the feast was placed on the table and all were seated, Jacob was asked to audibly say the blessing over the food. Before he began, he stood up and cleared his throat. "We have an extra special blessing to be thankful for this year. Besides a wonderful marriage, the Lord has chosen to bless me and Rachel with our first *boppli*!" His smile couldn't have stretched larger as he and Rachel received congratulations from the family.

Luke immediately looked to his wife and was saddened when he saw that her previously joyful countenance had fallen. *Lord, please help to heal Elisabeth's pain and help us to be thankful for the many blessings we do have.*

Carson moved the food around on his plate, occasionally taking a bite, but he hardly tasted any of his mother's delicious food. This Thanksgiving had been nothing like he planned. How had everything turned out so wrong? One minute, he and Elisabeth were the happiest couple in the world, both looking forward to spending the rest of their lives together. The next minute, their engagement was broken, the wedding called off, and he was heartbroken.

He couldn't stand being around the table a moment longer, especially when his brother sat happily across the table with his wife. First, he lost Brianna and now Elisabeth. There was nothing he could do about Brianna, but the complications with Elisabeth had been of his own making. Was it selfish to want Elisabeth all to himself? Probably. But he'd been around enough bratty kids to know he didn't want a houseful of them.

A sudden idea popped into his mind: Pastor Bill. Tomorrow he would go have a chat with their pastor. Perhaps he could help him work out this disagreement with Elisabeth and get her to see the light. After all, you don't just give a ring back because of one little argument. He was sure that this problem could be solved with the pastor's assistance.

Carson decided not to leave the table and became invigorated by his renewed sense of hope. Perhaps there was something concerning Elisabeth that he could be thankful for after all. He smiled slightly as he fingered the engagement ring that he'd carried around in his pocket since the day Elisabeth had given it back.

Elisabeth decided to forego preparing a Thanksgiving meal. After all, it was hardly worth it for just her and Samantha. So far, Samantha had been a pleasant roommate and they were becoming fast friends. She'd received an invitation to join Samantha and her family for Thanksgiving dinner, but had declined. She hadn't had much time for solitude, so this would be the perfect opportunity.

Now she sat all alone in her quiet apartment. Samantha had gone to her folks' place and Mattie and Richard were out of town visiting Richard's relatives. She figured Carson was probably enjoying a vegan Thanksgiving meal with his family. She sighed. Oh, how she wished things could be different between her and Carson, but they weren't. She knew that if it was God's will for them to be together that He would make a way.

What was her family doing back at home? She pictured *Dat* and *Mamm* smiling at each other while *Mamm* placed a large turkey on the table. Jacob, Michael, James, Tabitha, Paul, Martha, and Mary would all be gathered around the table. But there would be one empty spot: hers. She knew that her parents would always keep an open place for her at the table in hopes that she'd come back home. How her mother's heart must be breaking right now. For a moment, she could feel her pain.

Perhaps it was time to go back, at least for a visit. She would talk to her boss next week and see if maybe she could get a few days off of work. If for nothing else, it would do her good to get her mind off of Carson.

NINETEEN

"Hello, Mom," Ashley's voice sounded into the earpiece of Caroline's cell phone. "Have you been able to get any information from the airlines yet?"

Caroline sighed. "No, they keep giving me the runaround. They told me that a passenger flight list is strictly confidential and they are not allowed to release it due to privacy laws."

"Did you ask to speak to their superior?" Ashley huffed.

"I was talking to the superior, as far up as I could get."

"But did you tell them that you think your daughter was on the plane?" she said indignantly.

"Yes. They said that Brianna would absolutely have not been permitted to board without a passport," Caroline declared.

"So that means she wasn't on the plane!" Ashley exclaimed.

"It appears that way. But if she wasn't on the plane, where did she go?" she wondered aloud.

"She could still be alive, Mom. You don't think she would have run away, do you?" Ashley asked.

Caroline gasped. "Run away? She's twenty years old. Why would she run away?"

"I don't know. Yeah, I guess that does sound kind of silly. What if she was abducted?" Ashley knew she was grasping at straws, but what could explain her sister's sudden disappearance if she didn't die in that airplane crash? "I've got it! Carson! Didn't you say that he was with a woman who looked just like Brianna? Maybe it was her. Maybe he hypnotized her and told her that her name was now Elisabeth!"

"Ashley, that's absurd! Carson would never do anything like that," Caroline asserted.

"Are you one hundred percent certain that it wasn't her? You said that you and Dad both thought it was Brianna, that she was an exact double," she insisted. "If you don't get a hold of Carson, I will."

"I wish you wouldn't do that, Ashley."

"But Mom, maybe he has some clues. If nothing else, he'll probably help us look for her," Ashley said.

"All right, we can contact Carson. But please don't get the police involved, not yet anyway. Let's see what we can come up with on our own, and then if we still don't have answers we'll go to the authorities," Caroline said.

"I want to see this Elisabeth person. Does she really look that much like Brianna?" Ashley asked skeptically.

"Ashley, you have no idea." Caroline shook her head.

Elisabeth smoothed her dress and made sure her prayer *kapp* was on straight before she exited her driver's vehicle. She figured if she wanted her family to accept her, then she'd better at least look Amish, even if she wasn't. Besides, if she came to visit in her *Englischer* clothes, her parents would probably consider her disrespectful.

After the driver dropped her off at the end of the lane that led to her parents' home, she walked up the driveway taking in all the familiar scents and sites. The barn and house looked the same as it had when she left, apart from the snow that now covered the ground. The farm seemed unusually quiet, except for the sound of wood splitting.

Elisabeth strode up to the back porch and took a deep breath before she knocked, her confidence dwindling by the minute. *Will* Mamm *be happy to see me?* She hoped so. She knocked on the door, but no one answered. She knocked again. Nothing. *I guess I'll check the barn.*

On her way to the barn, she heard the sound of wood splitting again so she decided to check the woodshed first. She entered and quickly spotted her oldest brother Jacob. He had his sleeves rolled up to expose his muscled forearms and sweat dripped from his brow as he lifted the axe to slice through an oak log. Elisabeth smiled as she thought of her younger brother, now a man.

"Hi, Jacob," Elisabeth said sheepishly.

"Oh, *hullo*, Elisabeth." He wiped his brow, and then raised the axe again.

That's it? "That's all you're going to say?" Elisabeth stood bewildered.

"What? Are you expecting a party every time you come home?" Jacob lowered his eyebrows.

"No, but –"

"I've got work to do. This wood isn't going to cut itself," he insisted, turning back to the pile of unsplit logs.

Elisabeth couldn't believe his indifference about her return. He treated her as if he'd just seen her yesterday. "Do you know where *Mamm* is?"

"Yes, she and the others went into town. Shouldn't you be with Luke?" Jacob raised his eyebrows.

"I guess I'll go see him now. Tell *Mamm* I'll be back later." Elisabeth looked in bewilderment at her brother again, and then stalked off in the direction of Luke's place.

Carson patiently waited in a comfortable cloth-covered chair near the church secretary's desk. Pastor Bill had a prior meeting, but should be finishing up soon. He'd turned the volume off on his cell phone, but now it vibrated in his pocket. He stepped outside and tapped the screen on his phone to receive the call, although the number was unfamiliar.

"Hello?" Carson asked.

"Hello. Is this Carson?" a female voice said.

"Yes, who's calling?" Carson glanced through the window to make sure the pastor hadn't come out.

"This is Caroline Mitchell, Brianna's mother. Would you be able to meet with my daughter Ashley and me today? We have something that we'd like to discuss with you," Brianna's mom said.

"Sure. Where would you like to meet?" Carson tried to hurry along the conversation.

"How about Carl's Café at one o'clock?" Caroline suggested.

"That will work fine." Carson now spotted the pastor emerging from his office with a younger man.

"Thank you, goodbye."

Carson hung up and strolled back into the church's administrative building, wondering just what Brianna's mother and sister wanted to talk to him about. He greeted Pastor Bill with a handshake, and then followed him down a narrow hallway to his office. He smiled as he read a Bible verse someone had painted on the walls of the hallway, '...narrow is the way, which leadeth unto life, and few there be that find it.' He suddenly remembered his last conversation with Brianna, saddened that she never found the narrow way.

"Hello, Carson. I hope you're doing well." The pastor offered him the black leather seat across his desk and sat down in an identical chair on the other side.

Carson took a seat. "I'm all right. My fiancée and I had a disagreement and she gave me back my ring."

The pastor nodded and raised an eyebrow. "Is that what you'd like to discuss?"

"Yes, sir. You see, the disagreement was about having children. She used to be Amish, so I guess she wants a bunch of kids. I think one or two will be pushing it," Carson explained.

"I see. Well, it's a good thing that you want to work this out before you marry. Raising children is no small thing."

"I agree." Carson nodded, perusing the many bookshelves that lined the office walls.

"Have you ever considered where the Amish get their views on procreation?" Pastor Bill asked.

"No, not really. I thought they just want a bunch of kids so that they can help out with all the farm chores and keep the Amish traditions alive and well." He shrugged, and then laced his fingers together behind his head.

"While that may be part of it, that's not the main reason they tend to have so many children. Have you read Psalm one hundred twenty-seven?"

"I'm not sure. Probably."

Pastor Bill opened his Bible and read all five verses in the chapter. "First of all, this chapter talks about the Lord building the house. If we don't allow the Lord to build our house, then we are building in vain. In verse three, the psalmist says children are an heritage of the Lord. Heritage can also be defined as an inheritance, something passed down, and usually refers to a privilege or blessing." Carson nodded, indicating he understood, and the pastor continued, "And then He further states that the fruit of the womb is His reward. Verse five states that a man with a quiver full of arrows – or children – is a happy man."

"Whoa! Now that's a new take on things." Carson blew out a breath. "So, God wants us to have tons of children?"

"I think what God wants is for us to leave our lives in His hands and let Him make the decisions. We're supposed to allow God to build our house. God knows whether we can handle two or twelve children," Pastor Bill stated. "The problem is that we've become so entangled in the world and its philosophies that we have come to view children as a curse or a burden."

"When, in fact, they're supposed to be the opposite," Carson finished the pastor's sentiments.

"That is correct."

"So, I guess the question now is: Do I trust the Lord to build my house?" Carson pondered his own words. He abruptly stood up from the desk and held out his hand. "Thank you, Pastor. You've helped open my eyes." He laughed. "And I thought you were going to back me up so I could show Elisabeth she was wrong."

Pastor Bill laughed as well, shaking Carson's hand. "God's Word does put things in perspective, doesn't it?"

"It sure does." Carson smiled as he headed out the door. He prayed silently as he walked back to his car. *Lord, help me to trust You with my life.*

He had a couple of hours before his meeting with Caroline and Ashley, so he decided to swing by Elisabeth's apartment to discuss the meeting he had with Pastor Bill. Would she ever be happy!

Carson knocked on the door and Elisabeth's roommate answered.

"Oh, hello, Carson. Elisabeth isn't here, she went to Pennsylvania," Samantha informed him.

"Pennsylvania? She went back home?" Carson suddenly got a bad feeling in his gut. *What if she decides to stay? What if that Luke guy takes her back and she decides to marry him? I've got to go to Pennsylvania and bring her back home.*

"Do you have the address where she's staying?" Carson asked.

"Yes, let me write it down for you." She walked over to a desk in the living room and returned a few minutes later with a piece of paper in her hand.

He took the paper and glanced down at the information. "Thank you."

Carson hopped back in his car and determined what he should do. *I'll meet with Brianna's mother, and then I'll swing by the house and pick up a few things before I head out to Pennsylvania.*

Luke lifted his eyes and saw his beloved walking up the road toward him. He smiled. He never tired of seeing Elisabeth, but he was surprised to see her back home already. Since she was still a ways off, he figured he'd put the horse in the barn and give it some water to drink and fresh hay.

A few moments later, the barn door opened and Elisabeth slowly walked in. Luke closed the horse's stall door and turned to greet his wife. He walked up to her and took her in his arms, bending down to press his lips against her neck.

Elisabeth gasped and stepped back. "Luke."

"What's wrong? Aren't you happy to see me?" He looked into her eyes to identify the problem.

"Well, yes, but –" Elisabeth was interrupted by a voice coming from the barn door.

"Luke! What are you doing?" Brianna called out, her face ablaze with shock and hurt.

Luke stepped back and scratched his head. He looked at Elisabeth and then at Brianna. "What's going on?"

"That's what I'd like to know, Luke Beiler!" Brianna huffed.

"Elisabeth?" He looked at both of them.

"Yes?" Both women said at once.

"Huh?" Luke scratched his head, thoroughly confused. "Which of you is my *fraa*?"

Brianna gasped. "I am."

Elisabeth spoke up, "I don't know who *she* is, but I'm Elisabeth Schrock."

"But I'm Elisabeth Schrock, Elisabeth Beiler," Brianna asserted.

"You can't both be Elisabeth Schrock, that's impossible," Luke insisted.

"Okay, I think I know what's going on," Elisabeth stated. "Luke, this woman is an imposter."

Luke rubbed his forehead, still trying to get over the shock of not being able to tell who his wife was. "What are you talking about?"

"Yes, what are you talking about? I'm Luke's wife," Brianna declared proudly.

"I can prove that I'm Elisabeth Schrock. Luke, do you remember when I was in second grade and one of the Fisher brothers made me fall off the swing? You threatened to beat him up if he ever did it again. Or the time we ate so much popcorn and hot cocoa that we got so sick we both threw up?" Luke nodded his head and Elisabeth went on. "How about the time when you, me, and Jacob went sledding down that steep hill? Remember, we ended up hitting a tree? I still have the scar on my leg to prove it." Elisabeth pulled up her dress and pulled her sock down to show a two inch scar where the scrape had been.

"I don't understand. If you are Elisabeth," Luke turned to Brianna, "then who are you?"

"I'm Beth, your wife," Brianna asserted.

"No you are not! You are an imposter," Elisabeth's voice raised a notch as she glared at Brianna. She turned to Luke. "She's a fraud, Luke. I saw a report about this on television one time. She's one of those people who steals other women's identities. They study people who look like them, and then they pretend to be them and assume their identity. Sometimes they even get married so they can steal houses and real estate. They end up divorcing the poor spouse and leave them with nothing before they even know what's going on."

Divorce? Luke's heart sank. *I didn't really marry Elisabeth?* Luke looked at Elisabeth who stood glaring at an open-mouthed Brianna. Luke turned to Brianna and studied her. *Who is my wife? Could she be a pretender?* Luke thought about how she claimed she couldn't remember anything, and it all started making sense. "Who are you?" Suspicion overtook Luke as he looked into Brianna's eyes, firmly crossing his arms over his chest.

"I'm Elisabeth, your wife," she maintained.

Luke's voice rose as his anger flared, "No, she is Elisabeth!" He pointed to Elisabeth. "She's who I thought I'd married. What is your *real* name?" Luke demanded in a tone Brianna had never heard before.

Brianna's eyes filled with tears, fear tore at her heart. "I... I'm your wife." She trembled at the words she thought to be true. What else could she say?

Luke glared at her in disappointment. "You are not who I thought I married. You're not Elisabeth."

Brianna turned and fled from the barn, tears streaming down from her eyes.

Luke sank down onto a bale of hay, head in hands. *I've been betrayed.* That's all Luke could think of as he sat in stunned silence.

TWENTY

Carson stepped into the small coffee shop and quickly spotted Brianna's mother and sister. He walked over to their table with purpose and sat down across from the two ladies.

"Hello, Carson. Thank you for coming," Caroline said.

Carson nodded politely, but noticed Ashley giving him a strange look. "There was something you wanted to discuss?"

"Yes. You see, we don't think that Brianna was on Flight 245. We found her purse in her room and it still had her passport and identification in it. It appears she forgot it and her luggage at home," Caroline stated.

Carson's mouth hung open. "You mean..." He shook his head to try to gather his thoughts and process what he'd just been told. "But if she didn't get on the plane, then where did she go?"

"We were hoping you would know." Ashley's beady eyes stared him down.

"I have no idea. The last I saw her was when she left in the taxi." He shrugged, still not knowing what to think.

"That's it! The taxi!" Ashley proclaimed. "Maybe the cab driver abducted her."

Carson sat speechless, but Caroline spoke up, "Do you know which taxi she took to the airport? Maybe we can trace it."

Carson racked his brain for a name. "It was green and white. Hmm..."

"Budget Taxi Service," Ashley declared. "Yes, that's it. I'll call and see if anything suspicious happened on that day. They'll know whether one of their drivers disappeared or not."

"Ashley, I don't think she's been kidnapped." Her mother shook her head.

"Perhaps there was an accident," Carson suggested. "If Brianna didn't have any I.D. on her then they wouldn't have known who she was."

"She could be in a coma somewhere!" Ashley hollered.

"Ashley, calm down. You're drawing attention to our table," her mother admonished.

"I suppose she could be," Carson agreed.

"Why don't we call all of the hospitals and see if they have any patients who were admitted on the day Brianna disappeared. Hopefully, they'll be able to at least give us that information. And then we can go from there," Caroline suggested.

Carson rubbed his forehead wondering what he should do. "I wouldn't mind helping search, but I planned on going out of town and it's urgent. I'll have my cell phone with me if you need to get a hold of me."

Ashley eyed him suspiciously. "What are you going out of town for and where are you going?" She raised an eyebrow.

"Ashley!" Caroline spoke up. "I told you Carson doesn't have anything to do with Brianna's disappearance."

"Then why is he running off instead of helping us search for Brianna?" She squinted her eyes at him again.

"No, that's understandable," he said to Caroline. "Elisabeth and I had a disagreement and she called off the wedding. She went to Pennsylvania and I need to bring her back before I lose her."

Caroline patted Carson's hand. "I understand. Go ahead and go. Chances are, we'll find nothing anyway. We'll let you know if we do find something."

"Thank you," Carson said as he rose from the table. "I wish you God's blessing on your search. It would be wonderful if your daughter is still alive."

Brianna didn't know what else to do, so she ran as fast and hard as her legs would carry her. Where she was going, she had no idea. She just knew that she couldn't stay here.

Maybe she would go talk to Rachel. She had been a good friend to her since they met at the hospital, and now they were – well she thought they were – sisters-in-law. But Rachel had gone into Ronks with *Mamm* Schrock and the *kinner* today, so she wouldn't be home yet. Or perhaps she could go talk to Ruthie Spencer, another friend she had made while in Paradise. But would *they* only see her as a fake too? No more than a liar, like her husband now assumed she was?

Luke had turned his back on her – rejected her. How could he? How could this wonderful man that she had married choose someone else over his own wife? Because she was not Elisabeth Schrock. He thought he'd married Elisabeth Schrock and now he realized she was not her. Hadn't Luke loved *her* at all? Did he only marry her because of his past relationship with Elisabeth? Of course, he did.

How could she have been so blind? Because she had been desperate for love. So desperate for a place to belong that she didn't even think of the possibility that she might *not* be Elisabeth Schrock. After all, if Elisabeth's own family didn't even realize they were two different people then how could she have known?

How did Luke not know that she wasn't the real Elisabeth? It seemed to her that she and Elisabeth were as different as the sun and the moon. Had he been desperate too? After all, he'd waited years for Elisabeth's return.

It was clear now that Luke had only wanted Elisabeth for his wife. And now that she was back, his dreams could finally come true. The real Elisabeth could give him children. He had waited to marry Elisabeth and now she was his for the taking. It was obvious by the embrace that she'd seen them in that Luke still held a special place in Elisabeth's heart.

But if I'm not Elisabeth, then who am I? How will I ever be able to find out who I really am? Does anybody know my true identity?

Life was so unfair, so cruel. She had gone from someone who had nothing, who knew no one, to finding out that she was an Amish woman who had everything that really mattered. A loving family who wanted and cared for her and a man who she had grown to love and who she thought loved her as well. Now she was back where she started – all alone. But this time the pain was far worse. For she wasn't just alone now, she'd been rejected, unwanted by the man she loved more than life itself. And that was simply too much to bear.

Brianna's decision was made. She had to get away. She could only handle so much rejection. She needed to escape the agony and there was only one way she could think to do it. When she'd been in the hospital, they'd given her something to help her sleep. If she could just get a hold of more of those pills, the aching would go away. She knew the pain would never completely disappear, but it would help her to cope. And right now, that was all that she could ask for.

The first phone shanty she came to, she picked up the telephone and dialed the number of a driver. After agreeing to meet the driver in ten minutes, Brianna hurried out to the road that would take her to Lancaster. After that, she'd hire a taxi and go back to the hospital in New York. Perhaps they had answers, but if they didn't she knew they'd at least have something to help lessen the pain.

"Why are you here, Elisabeth? Did you just come back to ruin my life again?" Luke frowned.

"No. I wanted to come back and visit my family. I was kind of missing it, and because Carson and I were having some trouble. Oh, I don't know why I'm telling you all this." Elisabeth rolled her eyes.

"Who's Carson?" Luke crossed his arms.

"Carson is, or was, my fiancée," she explained.

"I should have known. Here, I waited for you and you were planning to marry someone else." He stomped his foot.

"Well, you got married to someone else," she said defensively.

"I thought I married you!" Luke paced back and forth. "You're right, you really are Elisabeth. And now that I think about it, I'm glad I didn't marry you. I'm glad I married Beth – uh, my wife. I can see now that you and she are quite different. You always have been selfish."

Elisabeth stood with her mouth agape, hurt etched in her pretty features. "So, you expected me to come back and marry you?"

"No." He shrugged. "But I'd hoped. You didn't say you were never coming back in your letter."

"I didn't know for sure. I thought that I would stay *Englisch*, but I'm a little confused now," Elisabeth admitted.

"Why did you leave in the first place?" Luke genuinely wondered.

"I told you in the letter that I felt I didn't fit in here. I wanted to try out the *Englisch* world before I made a commitment to remain Amish my entire life," she said. "I know I hurt you, Luke. I'm sorry about that."

"Jacob told me I shouldn't wait for you, but I'm glad I did. If I hadn't, I would have missed out on my wife." He realized.

"I can't believe there's another person who looks just like me. First, everyone thinks I look just like Brianna, who was evidently Carson's girlfriend. But I couldn't have been her because she died in a plane crash. Now, you marry this other woman – this fraud, this con artist – thinking she's me."

"Con artist? My wife can't be a fraud or con artist; she'd never do anything like that. She's not a liar. As a matter of fact, she's genuine and loving and…" Awareness dawned on Luke and his heart sank. "Oh no, what have I done?" He left Elisabeth in the barn and ran to the house.

"Beth! Beth! *Fraa!*" He searched the house frantically for Brianna. "*Lieb*, where are you?"

Elisabeth came to the door, out of breath. "What are you doing?"

"Looking for my wife!" He took his hat off and ran his fingers through his hair. Luke hung his head, shaking it in disbelief. *I've hurt her deeply.* "No, she can't be gone! I have to find her."

"Where would she be? Would she have gone to your mother's house?" Elisabeth asked.

"I don't know. I guess she could have gone to see Rachel." Luke surveyed the farm once more before deciding to hitch his buggy.

"I'll walk and cut through the field. I'll meet you at Rachel's house in a little while. Maybe one of us will see her if we go different ways," she suggested.

"You know that Rachel lives at your folks' place now, right?" Luke raised his eyebrows in question.

"Why would she live there?" she asked in surprise.

"Because she and your brother Jacob are married," he said, and then added with a smile, "and expecting a *boppli*."

"Really? Oh, that's wonderful!"

"Yes, well, you miss a lot when you're gone," Luke said, attempting to keep the edge of bitterness out of his voice.

"Apparently, I did." Elisabeth lifted an eyebrow. "By the way, Luke. Congratulations on your marriage. I hope you and your wife can work everything out. I guess I sort of ruined things for you."

"Thank you for saying that. My wife really is wonderful." He smiled. "We just need to find out who she actually is. I pray we can find her."

"I'll pray too," Elisabeth said, and then walked off in the direction of her parents' home.

As Luke set the buggy in motion, he prayed. *Lord, please help me find my wife. I don't know what I'd do without her. Apart from salvation, she's the best thing that's ever happened to me. I know I don't deserve her, but I love her, Lord. I can't lose her.* Tears clouded Luke's eyes, so that he couldn't see the road ahead. Thankfully, his horse knew the way. *Please don't let me lose her...*he couldn't continue his prayer, for the thought of losing her was too overwhelming.

TWENTY-ONE

The driver Brianna hired had dropped her off in Lancaster as requested. She now waited for the taxi she had called and was relieved when it showed up before anyone else from the Amish community did. The last thing she needed was another person coming to accuse her of fraud. Who knows, maybe Elisabeth decided to call the police to have her arrested. All Brianna knew is that she had to flee as soon as possible.

Now that she knew she wasn't Elisabeth Schrock, she presumed her roots could not be Amish. She had met Rachel at the hospital in New York, and while there were some Amish in the state, there weren't many. She figured she must be an *Englischer*.

When she stepped into the taxi cab, a familiar feeling came over her sending chills up her spine. Had she been here before?

"Where to, miss?" The driver looked back at her over his shoulder and immediately she pictured another man. It was only a split second, but the sudden image that flashed in her mind kindled familiarity. Was it the man who had perished in the accident? Could it be that her memory was returning?

"Saint Luke's Hospital, New York City," *How ironic*, she thought wryly. Saint Luke. That was exactly how she'd felt about him. Oh, how she missed Luke already! But no, he had rejected her. Luke didn't want her anymore. Only one person held a place in his heart. Elisabeth.

She must find out who she really is. Only then could she attempt to find her real family and the life that was truly hers.

"Do you mind if I turn on the radio?" the driver asked.

A sudden wash of memories came over Brianna at his words, but in bits and pieces...*plane crash...Heidi...passport... God.* What did it all mean? She hit the side of her head with her palm, attempting to jar her memory. *Plane crash...plane crash...plane crash. I got it! I was supposed to be on a plane that crashed. Or was someone else on the plane that crashed? Heidi, maybe?* She didn't know for sure, but at least she was beginning to remember something.

The ride to the hospital seemed a lot shorter than it actually was. She had been lost in her thoughts, trying to force the memories of Luke and the Amish community out of her head, but it hadn't worked. She stepped out of the car and glanced up at the large sign bearing the hospital's, and her husband's, name. The aching that gripped her heart overwhelmed her. She arrived at the nurses' station and immediately recognized some of the women behind the counter. Her hands began shaking and she suddenly felt weak and lightheaded.

"Hello, may I help you?" a voice called from behind a window.

Brianna didn't know how or if she responded, but she woke up in a hospital bed. As she blinked her eyes, she tried to figure out what had happened. She coughed, automatically bringing her hand to her mouth, and that's when she noticed the IV needle in her hand. A nurse walked in bearing a tray of food. Just then, she remembered she hadn't eaten since...*since when?* It must've been the early morning breakfast with Luke, but even then she didn't eat much because she hadn't been very hungry.

"Let's get some food into you, shall we?" The nurse set the tray on the bedside table and wheeled it to Brianna.

"What happened? Why am I here?" Brianna asked.

"You came up to the nurses' station, and then you passed out cold. We're not exactly sure why, so the doc ordered some tests. I'm suspecting it's a lack of food, though. Are you anemic or hypoglycemic maybe?" She lifted her brow.

"I don't know."

"Well, I guess they'll figure all that out when they receive your test results." The nurse checked the contents of the IV bag that hung from a mobile metal stand.

"Could I get some sleeping pills?" Brianna blurted out.

"Sleeping pills? Are you having trouble sleeping?" The nurse threw her a skeptical look.

"Uh...yeah," she lied.

"I'll see what I can do." Before the nurse walked out of the room, she called over her shoulder, "I'll bring some paperwork by when I come back in."

Brianna took a deep breath, and then lay back against the hospital bed. *I can't believe I'm here again.* She picked up the sandwich on the plate in front of her and took a bite. She chewed, but tasted nothing. *Where am I going to go from here?* She'd hoped that more of her memory would return, but it hadn't. *Lord, it would be nice to at least know who I am,* she silently pleaded. It was then that she realized that she still had God. He was the only one who hadn't left her. He knew who she was, even if she didn't. A single tear formed in the corner of her eye as she thanked God for not abandoning her – especially when she needed Him most.

Carson's platinum Volvo S80 pulled up to a large white clapboard farmhouse with green shutters. He looked around the quaint setting before sliding out of the car. He had seen photos of Amish farms before, but had never visited one personally. The massive barn was overwhelming and he couldn't help but imagine how dangerous it must've been to build. Had Elisabeth's community built this gigantic barn for her family at a barn raising? Or had it been in the family for generations, possibly built by a great-grandfather? One wouldn't be able to tell by just looking because it appeared to have a fresh coat of paint and they'd kept the same style of barn for centuries.

A large snow-covered pasture stood empty and Carson surmised that, had it been spring time, cattle and horses would be happily grazing in the now-barren field. Had Elisabeth worked on this farm with her seven siblings, from sunup to sundown? Did she run and play in this pasture as a child? A smile tugged at his lips as he pictured her as a little Amish girl, so cute.

He walked up the porch steps to the front door and knocked. It had taken a few minutes, but an Amishman near his own age gingerly answered the door. Carson assumed he was newly married because he wore a short beard.

"Do you need something?" the man asked curiously.

Carson guessed that they didn't receive many *Englisch* callers. He moved his sunglasses to the top of his head. "Yes, actually. I'm looking for Elisabeth Schrock."

"Who are you?" the suspender-clad man asked cautiously.

"I'm sorry, my name is Carson. Carson Welch. I'm a friend of Elisabeth's." He held out his hand and the young Amishman offered a firm handshake.

"*Kumm.*" He turned and led the way through the house. Carson noticed the walls were plain and bare, remembering how Elisabeth told him the Amish did not approve of photographs, equating them to graven images. The furnishings in the spacious living room were simple, with a couch, a rocking chair, and a straight-back oak chair. A small handcrafted table inhabited the space between the two chairs and a hand-crocheted rag rug lay on the floor between the couch and chairs. With the fireplace ablaze, a cozy feeling came over him as he pictured a family gathered together in the room.

They passed through a doorway and came into another room. Elisabeth sat at long table near the kitchen with another woman and young Amishman.

Elisabeth looked up in surprise. "Carson?"

"I'm sorry that I didn't let you know I was coming. I guess your cell phone is off and I don't have a number for here. Samantha gave me the address," he explained.

She looked up at him questioningly. "Why are you here?" He caught the hopefulness in her eye.

Carson gulped. He really didn't want to discuss something so personal in front of a bunch of strangers. "Can we talk? Alone, I mean."

"Actually, we were just discussing something really important." Elisabeth must've noticed his discomfort, because she stood up and went to his side. "Let me introduce you to everyone. This is my brother Jacob." She pointed to the man who'd opened the door. "This is his wife Rachel. And Luke, a friend of the family."

Carson knew the name, and wasn't thrilled that she'd been sitting at the table next to him. Nevertheless, he nodded politely.

"Have a seat. Would you like some coffee?" Elisabeth offered as she went to the stove.

He nodded and then took a seat near Luke, who seemed distraught. It was then Carson noticed faint blond whiskers on Luke's face. Was he married?

When Elisabeth returned to the table, she eyed Luke. "Do you mind if I tell him?" Luke shook his head.

She focused on Carson. "It's kind of a long story. You see, back in July, Rachel met a woman at St. Luke's Hospital in New York who looked just like me. So much so, that she thought she actually was me. But the woman had been in a car accident and couldn't remember who she was. Rachel, thinking the woman was me, brought her home to my family. Luke and she married a little over a month ago. When I came home, I thought she was an imposter, someone trying to steal my identity. And then she –"

Carson placed his hands on the table and abruptly stood up. "It's Brianna, I'm sure of it."

"Brianna?" Luke's eyes lifted.

"But I thought Brianna was dead? I thought she died in a plane crash," Elisabeth asked, confusion marring her face.

"So did I. And her parents did too. See, her mother hadn't gone into her room since before the crash. I guess she just didn't want to deal with the painful memories. When she finally did, she discovered Brianna's passport and identification in her bedroom. She called the airlines and they confirmed her theory that Brianna would not have been allowed to board the airplane without her passport, so we figured something else must've happened to her."

Rachel spoke up, "She said she had been in a terrible accident and couldn't remember who she was when she woke up from her coma. The nurses informed her that the taxi cab driver had died, but since she had no identification on her they simply called her Jane Doe."

"So, where is she now?" Carson asked.

"We don't know." Luke's countenance fell and his eyes misted. It was clear that he loved his wife and missed her. "We've searched all around Paradise, but have come up with nothing. None of our friends and neighbors have seen or heard from her." Desperation was evident in Luke's shaky voice.

"She didn't know anybody else. The only placed she'd been other than here, was the hospital," Rachel commented. "Do you think maybe she might have gone back there?"

"That'd be our best bet," Carson agreed. "I'll call her parents and suggest they go there immediately."

Luke spoke, holding up a trembling hand. "Before we do anything, can we pray?" Everybody agreed and they all bowed their heads in silent prayer.

Carson silently thanked God that Brianna was alive and had a husband who turned to God in time of need. *Had Brianna finally learned to trust in God?* Carson prayed it was so.

TWENTY-TWO

*B*rianna sat up in her hospital bed, attempting to fill in the form the nurse had brought. She looked down at the paper on the clipboard. *Name. Address. Date of birth. Phone number.* She sighed. Should she put down Elisabeth Beiler? No, that was not her name. Should she write Luke's address and the telephone number for the phone shanty? Another tear formed in her eye then slid down her cheek. This was all so frustrating. She just didn't know what to write.

Maybe she would write Mrs. Beiler. After all, she was still Luke's wife. But would he still want her? She knew she wasn't Elisabeth, but perhaps Luke could learn to love *her*. If she went home, would he take her back and allow her to be his wife once again? Bishop Hostettler did say that the bonds of marriage could only be broken by death. But what if you married somebody by accident? What if you married someone thinking they were somebody else? Did the rules still apply then? Deep inside, she hoped they did.

She was afraid to go back home, though. Afraid of Luke's rejection. Fearful of her – or Elisabeth's – family's rejection. Did they all now think she was a liar, some con artist trying to steal their fortune, as Elisabeth implied?

As she struggled with her thoughts, the door to her room opened. But instead of the nurse entering, two *Englischer* women with surprised and hopeful expressions came to her bedside. One woman was older, about the age of *Mamm* Schrock, and the other was around her own age. Both women looked familiar. *So familiar.* Did she know them?

"Brianna!" The older woman flew to her bedside and engulfed her in a hug.

"Mom?" She wasn't sure why she said the name, but she sensed it might be true.

"Yes!" Tears flowed from her mother's eyes. "Yes. Do you remember me?"

"I'm not sure," Brianna answered hesitantly. "You both look so familiar."

"Hello, Brianna." The other woman gingerly came forward. "I'm Ashley, your older sister."

"My name is Brianna?" The name held a familiar ring, more so than 'Elisabeth' had.

"Yes, Brianna Mitchell," her mother informed her.

"That would be Brianna Beiler now," she informed them. "I'm married."

Her mother looked at her sister and gasped in surprise. "Married? How could that be?"

"It's a really long story. How did you find me here?"

"Oh, honey! We thought you died in a plane crash. You were on your way to Germany to visit Heidi and when we heard the plane had gone down, we were devastated." Her mother brushed away tears. "You see, I couldn't bear the thought of entering your room to sort through your belongings. We just recently discovered that you'd left your passport and identification in your room at home. That's when we learned you were never on that plane and that something else must've happened to you."

"Now it all makes sense." Brianna rubbed her head.

"We told Carson about it too. He's in Pennsylvania. He called and informed us that you might be here so we came immediately," her mother said.

"Carson?" The name did sound vaguely familiar.

"He was your boyfriend before the plane crash," Ashley informed her sister.

"Oh no."

"He's engaged now," she added quickly, "supposedly to someone who looks just like you."

"Elisabeth Schrock?" Brianna's eyes widened.

"Yes, how did you know?" Her mother's expression was just as bewildering as her own must be.

"This is so strange. Oh wow. I can't believe this." Brianna's head spun. "Elisabeth was Luke's girlfriend before she left the Amish. Luke Beiler is my husband. It's almost as if we switched places."

"That is simply amazing, unbelievable really," Ashley said with eyes wide.

"How did you meet your husband?" her mother asked.

"Rachel, an Amish woman and good friend of mine now, saw me here at the hospital and thought I was Elisabeth Schrock. She brought me home to Pennsylvania and Luke and I fell in love. Well, I thought he fell in love with me," she said, sniffling, "but I don't know now. Everything is so confusing."

Her mother patted her arm, reassuringly. "I'm sure it will all work out. You don't need to talk about this now. Would you like to come home with us? I think seeing some of your old familiar surroundings may help you remember. I've already spoken to the nurse and she said you're ready to discharge."

"I'd love to come home with you, Mom." She gave her mother a hug and smiled. It felt like such a relief to finally learn her true identity. "Thank you. Now that I know who I am, I think I might be able to fill out these forms better."

"I have to go to New York. I need to bring my wife – Brianna – back home," Luke insisted, rising from the table.

"I'll take you there. My car is just outside," Carson suggested.

Luke nodded and grabbed his black woolen felt hat off the rack, placing it on his head.

"Elisabeth, why don't you come with us?" Carson suggested. "We still need to talk. And it will be interesting to see you and Brianna side by side to see how much you actually look alike."

"I was hoping to see my parents," she said reluctantly.

"You can see them when we bring Luke and Brianna back home. Would that suit you?" Carson asked, and then longingly gazed into her eyes. "I'd hoped to speak with you now, but it can wait until we find some time alone."

"Yes, I'll come. Jacob, tell *Mamm* and *Dat* I'll be back," Elisabeth said.

Jacob nodded and then watched the three of them walk out the door.

Brianna glanced around her old bedroom, taking in her surroundings, thankful to have some time to herself. It was so familiar, yet seemed so far away. Her memories had not come rushing back like she thought they would. Instead, things just seemed vaguely familiar.

On her large bed was a beautiful silk comforter in deep red. Matching valances hung in the two windows. A door led to a small bathroom and another one to a large walk-in closet. Her mother had informed her that all her clothing had been boxed up. She looked into some of the boxes and pulled out an outfit, trying it on. She stared at herself – Brianna – in a full length mirror that hung on the closet door. The jeans and sweater felt so different than the cape dress she'd become so accustomed to wearing.

She looked at some pictures that were held in wooden frames on the dresser. She, with her father, mother, and sister stood in front of the Statue of Liberty when she was twelve years old. She and Heidi sat near where the Twin Towers of the World Trade Center once stood. She and Carson, she surmised, in a strip of black and white photos from a photo booth. He was good-looking, she had to admit. But he definitely wasn't Luke.

She sank down on her old bed and wept into her pillow. Would she and Luke ever be the same again? Was he still upset that she wasn't who he thought she was? Did he still believe she was just an imposter? Perhaps God could work this for good somehow. She knelt beside her bed and began to pray.

A knock on the door interrupted her prayer. She sighed, wiping her tears, and then opened the door. *Luke*!

Luke grasped the door frame to steady himself when the door to Brianna's bedroom opened. There stood his wife, so beautiful, so enticing, and so disheartened. Oh, if he could only take back the words he'd last said to her! He'd prayed the whole trip over here, begging God to place forgiveness in her heart.

Would she want to come back to him? Or now that she knew she was *Englisch,* would she want to stay here in the city with her real family? Uncertainty filled his heart. Had he ruined everything?

"Brianna?" He opened his arms and released an anxious sigh when Brianna melted into him. He kissed the top of her head and held her tight, never wanting to let her go.

"Please forgive me," his voice quavered.

Brianna looked into his eyes and couldn't speak for tears of joy. A moment later, she responded, "Oh, Luke! I...I didn't think you still wanted me."

Her words brought sorrow to his heart. "I'm sorry, *Lieb*. I'm so sorry. I want you, of course I want you. I can't imagine being without you." He pressed his mouth to hers, and she fervently returned his delicious kisses. "Come home with me."

TWENTY-THREE

Dying for some fresh air, Elisabeth sat on the front steps of the Mitchells' upscale suburban home. It was every bit as fancy as the home Carson lived in and she could see how Brianna's and his families would have a lot in common, unlike her and Carson. Not that her family was dirt poor, but their worlds just seemed so far apart; the childrearing issue being only one difference.

She knew she'd never go back to being Amish. But what if she decided she couldn't live in The Big Apple? The trip back to Lancaster made her realize that she was a country girl through and through. Her apartment already felt too confining. There were so many things to think about.

Carson popped his head out the door. "I thought I'd find you out here."

"I needed some fresh air," she stated.

Carson joined her on the steps. "Isn't it great that Brianna and Luke were able to work things out?" He waited for her response.

"Yes. It's wonderful. I guess I messed things up for them." Elisabeth sighed.

"Not really. God has a way of making things work out. If you hadn't shown up in Pennsylvania, Brianna's disappearance would still be a mystery. Her family is thankful to have her back – even if she is Amish now." He chuckled. "Never in a million years would I have imagined Brianna becoming Amish. At least Luke knows his wife's real name now."

"I guess people change." She shrugged.

"Yes, they do." Carson took Elisabeth's hand in his. "That is why I went to Pennsylvania to find you. I – or I should say God – changed my mind about having children. Pastor Bill helped me to see that I need to trust God in every aspect of my life, including the childbearing department. The world is so different when viewed through the light of God's Word."

"Yes, it is," she agreed.

Carson pulled the ring out of his pocket and held it in his hand. "If you'll have me, I'd still like to become your husband." He held out the ring for her to take.

She stared down at the ring. "So you don't mind having fifteen children?" She eyed him suspiciously.

"If that's what the Lord wants, then no, I don't," he insisted.

"But what about other things? We're just so different. What if I want to live in the country?" she protested.

"What if *I* want to live in the country?" He raised his eyebrows.

"You do?" She waited for his nod. "Really?"

Carson nodded again. "I wouldn't mind. After visiting your home, I can see how you'd want to live in a similar environment."

She looked down at the ring in Carson's hand and smiled. "I'd love to marry you."

Carson leaned over and kissed her, and then placed the ring back on her finger. "What do you think about eloping?"

"Eloping? Are you serious?" Her eyes widened. "But I already have my dress."

"Which makes it perfect. You can wear your dress. We can invite whoever you'd like. But let's not wait until spring. I'd like to get married before Christmas. What do you say?" He smiled hopefully.

"But what about Hawaii?" she argued.

"The tickets are refundable, but I think all we need to do is change the date. We'd be going sooner. And the weather in Maui is nice all year round." He came close and whispered in her ear, "We could be on our honeymoon two weeks from now."

"I say yes," she answered calmly.

"You say yes?" Carson repeated excitedly.

She wrapped her arms around him, faced him nose to nose, and smiled. "Yes!"

Luke grabbed the pitchfork and climbed the ladder to the haymow. He removed four flakes of alfalfa from the bale, and then descended the ladder in record speed. After plunking a forkful of hay down for Popcorn, the mare that pulled the buggy, he moved on to Gladiator's stall.

A shrill ring broke through the wintry silence and Luke ambled out to the phone shanty, trudging through the snow. They didn't receive many calls and when they did, it was usually regarding something important. He picked up the receiver and answered.

"Hello, may I speak with Brianna Beiler please?" the professional sounding female voice asked.

Luke smiled. He still loved hearing his wife's name in conjunction with his surname. "*Jah.* I will get her. You will have to wait a little bit, because she is in the house."

Luke ran back up to the house and spotted his wife in the kitchen. He noticed it would take Brianna a while to don her snow boots since she was wearing her normal footwear. Without a word, he scooped her up into his arms and carried her outside.

Brianna laughed after she caught her breath. "Whatever are you doing, Luke?"

He smiled as he tromped through the fresh powder, carrying her in his strong arms. "You have a telephone call. I thought it would be faster this way."

"Who is it?" she wondered aloud.

"I don't know. They didn't say and I didn't ask." He shrugged, and then set her down inside the shanty.

Brianna picked up the line. "Hello. This is Brianna."

"Hello, Brianna. This is Norma Hutchins calling from Saint Luke's Hospital." The woman paused.

Brianna covered the mouthpiece and waved Luke closer. "It's Saint Luke's Hospital."

He looked at her in concern, and then placed his ear next to hers so he could listen to the conversation.

"The reason I called is to inform you of your test results," the nurse said.

"I already received the test results," Brianna informed the woman. "They confirmed that I was anemic."

"Yes, that's correct. But in light of your pregnancy, the doctor is recommending an iron supplement," Norma stated.

Luke and Brianna stared at each other in confusion. "I'm sorry; I don't think I heard you correctly. Could you repeat what you just said?" Brianna asked.

"I said in light of your pregnancy –"

"I'm sorry, you must be mistaken." Brianna hung her head. "I'm not pregnant. I'm not able to have children. The doctor told me that I'm incapable of conceiving." A tear formed in her eye and Luke pulled her close.

"No. I have the results right here in front of me. You are Brianna Beiler, correct?"

"Yes."

"The urine sample you left us indicates that you are definitely pregnant," Nurse Norma said emphatically.

Brianna's eyes widened and Luke smiled. "I…I am?"

"Yes, most definitely, but if you'd like to check for yourself, you can take a home pregnancy test. I'm sure it will confirm our results. These tests are ninety-nine point nine percent accurate," the nurse asserted.

"Oh, wow. I'm pregnant!" She smiled, jumped up and down, and kissed Luke. "I'm pregnant! We're going to have a baby!"

Luke took her into his arms and kissed her back. "Yes, I guess we are."

"Uh, hello?" the phone called out.

Luke quickly picked up the phone. "Hi. I'm sorry. My wife's just a little excited. We will make sure that she gets plenty of iron. Thank you for calling." He hung the phone back onto its cradle.

"Can you believe it, Luke? Our very own *boppli*!" Brianna was overjoyed.

Luke scooped Brianna back up into his arms; a tear glistened in his eye. "With all that God has done in our lives, I can believe anything. I have been blessed beyond measure."

EPILOGUE

Thanksgiving Day, seven years later…

 *B*rianna shifted the sleeping infant in her arms and pulled the blanket around the small bundle tighter. A buzzer sounded in the kitchen and she rose to take baby Beth to her father on the couch.

Carson smiled fondly and received his tiny little girl. "Are you sure you wouldn't like to hold her longer?"

Brianna smiled as Elisabeth looked tenderly at her daughter and husband. Who would have thought they'd already have six children after only seven years of marriage? "No, I have to take the turkey out of the oven. Jacob and Rachel should be arriving with their little ones any moment. Perhaps you, Luke, and Jacob can take all our *kinner* outside to play until the rest of the dinner is ready."

"That sounds like fun. I think I'll join Luke outside in just a bit. Right now I want to cherish this one a bit longer." Carson smiled and wrapped his arm around Elisabeth, cradling the baby in his other arm.

"I always knew you'd make a good daddy." Elisabeth leaned over and kissed her husband's cheek.

The back door blew open and Luke bustled in with Jacob, Rachel, and their three *kinner*. The children shot out of the kitchen in short order, probably in search of their cousins.

"Somethin' smells *appeditlich, Schweschder!*" Jacob bellowed as he wrapped Brianna in a hug.

"Hey now." Luke warned teasingly. "She's not your sister, but she is *my* wife. Hands off."

Jacob smiled, holding up his hands in mock surrender, and then chuckled. "Well, now that I think of it that might work out *gut*. Since we're not related in any way, our *kinner* could marry someday."

"Yes, but since they are so close they'll think they're cousins and they won't want to." Rachel smiled and set a casserole on the counter. She placed a hand on her rounded belly. Baby number four was expected to arrive in two months.

Brianna turned around and placed a large knife in Jacob's hand. "*Denki, Bruder,* for volunteering to carve the turkey."

"But I didn't –" Jacob protested.

"Now, now, Jacob. Think of the benefits. You get to be the first one to taste test the bird." Brianna nonchalantly removed the knife from his hand and shrugged, hiding a wry smile. "Unless, of course, if you don't know how to do it…"

"Give that back to me." He grabbed the knife.

"Hey, what's all the commotion in here?" Elisabeth asked as she and Carson joined the group in the kitchen.

"Your brother here was just saying he didn't know how to carve a turkey," Brianna teased.

"I did no such thing!" Jacob snapped.

"Calm down, Jake. Can't you tell when Brianna's teasing you? I'd think you'd be used to it by now," Elisabeth said, giving her brother and his wife a hug.

"So, how long do we have before the meal is ready?" Carson asked, holding his squirming one-year-old son.

"I'd say about twenty minutes," Brianna responded. "I think Luke has the sleigh readied. Why don't you men take the *kinner* for a short ride in the cutter as soon as Jacob's finished carving the turkey? We girls can stay here with the *bopplin* and get dinner on the table."

"That sounds like a *gut* plan," Luke spoke up, and then kissed his wife before heading out the door. The other men shortly followed suit, leaving the womenfolk alone to talk.

"Let me see that adorable little *boppli*," Rachel squealed, walking over to Elisabeth and peeking into the pink fleece.

"I can't get over how precious each new life is. God sure has blessed Carson and me. And he's turned out to be such a fine father." Elisabeth beamed, holding out the baby. "Would you like to hold her?"

Rachel happily took the bundle from Elisabeth's arms and cooed over the babe. "I can't believe our little Jake is almost three. I'm more than ready for a new infant in the house."

"I know what you mean," Brianna spoke quietly, gauging her friends' response. "I'm thankful for our two, but I'm thrilled that God is blessing us with another one next year."

"Oh, Brianna, really?" Rachel beamed.

"That's wonderful!" Elisabeth added.

Brianna placed a finger over her lips. "Shh...Luke doesn't know yet. I'm planning to surprise him with the news today."

Elisabeth stood at the back door, peering through the window. The three men and ten children all wore happy smiles and pink cheeks as they maneuvered the horse and sleigh back toward the barn. "You'd better get that hot cocoa out because they'll be back in really soon. They just pulled up to the barn."

Brianna surveyed the long wooden table filled with delicious bounty. Turkey, mashed potatoes and gravy, green bean casserole, potato rolls, and cranberry sauce enveloped her senses. Carson and Elisabeth had brought along a couple of vegan dishes as well. "I think everything is on the table and ready to go. We just need some hungry mouths to feed."

Rachel laughed. "I don't think you'll have any trouble with that. Jacob could probably tackle this table on his own. Sometimes I think that man has a hollow leg."

"Make that two!" Jacob called from the door, leading a line of children to the sink to wash up.

Rachel shook her head. "I don't know how he does that. He must have ESPN or something."

Carson and the other men roared with laughter. "I think what you meant to say is ESP. ESPN is a television sports station."

"Whatever!" Rachel capitulated.

"Yeah, if I had ESPN I'd probably be receiving a visit from Deacon Yoder!" Jacob teased, kissing his wife's head.

"Enough of the banter. Let's all take our seats and thank the Lord for his bountiful blessings," Luke advised thoughtfully.

Each person found a place at the table in no particular order. However, the parents sat next to their littlest ones. Luke bowed his head for the silent prayer and everyone followed suit. When he lifted his head, he made a suggestion. "Since we're all gathered together here this year, I'd like to start a new tradition. Let's each one say what we're most thankful for."

The sea of family and friends seated at the table nodded in unison. A couple of the oldest children grumbled, but quickly submitted after a reproving look from a parent. After each one reverently gave their thanks, all eyes turned to Brianna at last.

"I'd like to thank God for giving me eternal life, a wonderful family, great friends, and for the new *boppli* Luke and I will have next year." Her countenance glowed when she observed Luke's surprised but pleased expression. "And even though I may have become Amish by accident, I know that God opened my eyes to His love on purpose. And for that I will forever be thankful."

The End

Amish Secrets - Book 1

An **Unforgivable** Secret

J.E.B. Spredemann

*H*annah has a good life. A beautiful home, a loving husband, and a wonderful Amish community are only a few of her daily blessings. But she has carried a heavy burden for years: a secret that no one must know. When tragedy strikes, her secret threatens to be revealed, jeopardizing everything she's ever loved. Will Hannah be able to face her greatest fear and find God's purpose for her life?

Inspirational Christian Fiction Approx. 250 pages

An Unforgivable Secret

AMISH SECRETS - BOOK 1

J.E.B. Spredemann

PROLOGUE

*I*t is a secret I intend to keep buried forever. But like all secrets, it begs to be told. Nobody knows. Only me. And if I had my way, not even I would know. The secret is powerful. It has the potential to destroy my life. On the other hand, if revealed, could it possibly bring a sense of peace to my soul? But I will never tell a soul. Ever.

Amish Girls Series - Book 1

Joanna's
Struggle

J.E.B. Spredemann

*U*ntil the day Joanna Fisher attends a Mud Sale with her family, she lives a typical eleven-year-old Amish girl's life. She attends a one-room school house with her siblings and friends, works on the family farm, and spends her free time riding her beautiful blue-eyed horse, Blueberry. But when something unexpected happens at the Mud Sale, Joanna's world is turned upside-down. Can one event change the course of her life forever? Approximately 100 pages.

Life, Love, and Friendship...
the *Amish Girls Series* for teens

Available now at online retailers

CPSIA information can be obtained at www.ICGtesting.com
Printed in the USA
BVOW05s1921010415

394245BV00002B/93/P